"For A Moment, You Looked At Me As A Man, Not A Prince,"

Prince Michel said, in a voice like velvet.

Maggie's chest squeezed tight with an emotion she couldn't name. Closing her eyes, she tried to take a deep breath to dispel it.

"Didn't you?" he asked.

"What if I did?" she retorted, but the breathy sound in her voice diminished the punch of her words.

"Open your eyes," he told her.

She automatically did as he commanded, then frowned. "You give a lot of orders."

"I want to kiss you," he said, not taking his gaze from hers.

Before she could do more than stare in surprise, he slid his hand around the nape of her neck and took her mouth with his.

Pleasure taunted her. *It's just a kiss*, she told herself.

But he's a prince.

Not at this moment....

Dear Reader,

Welcome to Silhouette Desire, where every month you can count on finding six passionate, powerful and provocative romances.

The fabulous Dixie Browning brings us November's MAN OF THE MONTH, *Rocky and the Senator's Daughter,* in which a heroine on the verge of scandal arouses the protective *and* sensual instincts of a man who knew her as a teenager. Then Leanne Banks launches her exciting Desire miniseries, THE ROYAL DUMONTS, with *Royal Dad,* the timeless story of a prince who falls in love with his son's American tutor.

The Bachelorette, Kate Little's lively contribution to our 20 AMBER COURT miniseries, features a wealthy businessman who buys a date with a "plain Jane" at a charity auction. The intriguing miniseries SECRETS! continues with *Sinclair's Surprise Baby,* Barbara McCauley's tale of a rugged bachelor with amnesia who's stunned to learn he's the father of a love child.

In *Luke's Promise* by Eileen Wilks, we meet the second TALL, DARK & ELIGIBLE brother, a gorgeous rancher who tries to respect his wife-of-convenience's virtue, while *she* looks to *him* for lessons in lovemaking! And, finally, in Gail Dayton's delightful *Hide-and-Sheikh,* a lovely security specialist and a sexy sheikh play a game in which both lose their hearts...and win a future together.

So treat yourself to all six of these not-to-be-missed stories. You deserve the pleasure!

Enjoy,

Joan Marlow Golan

Joan Marlow Golan
Senior Editor, Silhouette Desire

Please address questions and book requests to:
Silhouette Reader Service
U.S.: 3010 Walden Ave., P.O. Box 1325, Buffalo, NY 14269
Canadian: P.O. Box 609, Fort Erie, Ont. L2A 5X3

Royal Dad
LEANNE BANKS

Published by Silhouette Books
America's Publisher of Contemporary Romance

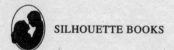 **SILHOUETTE BOOKS**

ISBN 0-373-76400-6

ROYAL DAD

Copyright © 2001 by Leanne Banks

Visit Silhouette at www.eHarlequin.com

Printed in U.S.A.

Books by Leanne Banks

LEANNE BANKS

a bestselling author of romance, lives in her native Virginia with her husband, son and daughter. Recognized for both her sensual and humorous writing with two Career Achievement Awards from *Romantic Times Magazine,* Leanne likes creating a story with a few grins, a generous kick of sensuality and characters that hang around after the book is finished. Leanne believes romance readers are the best readers in the world because they understand that love is the greatest miracle of all. Contact Leanne online at leannebbb@aol.com or write to her at P.O. Box 1442, Mid-lothian, VA 23113. A SASE for a reply would be greatly appreciated.

Special acknowledgments to the
Lindamood-Bell Reading Clinic for their creative
and exciting techniques for helping people learn to read.

This book is dedicated to all the special education
reading teachers who go the extra mile to help
nonreaders become readers. Thank you.

Prologue

He needed a wife.

The assignment was long overdue. Michel had put it off as long as possible. Leaning against his balcony rail, he looked at the private courtyard shimmering in moonlight. He knew the requirements for the position: discretion, grace, understanding and respect for his position. According to his advisors, a woman who provided a politically beneficial association would be a plus.

Michel's wife had passed away years ago, leaving him to parent his son by himself. With a dull pang, he remembered fragile Charisse. She had been a conscientious wife and loving mother. Although

Charisse had been chosen for him, or perhaps *because* she had been chosen for him, Michel had never felt more than a gentle fondness and protectiveness for his late wife. His son had suffered most from her death.

Even now, Michel's advisors had one list of requirements for the type of woman he should marry; Michel had another. He was older now and not as inclined to accept his advisors' choice as the final word for him. Whoever he married would love his son as if he were her own child.

If he were to place an order for a wife, he would say he preferred a woman with silky, long black hair and a body with well-proportioned curves. He preferred a woman with a quiet voice and a soft laugh and, most important, a biddable nature.

He moved his hand, and the moonlight reflected the gold ring on his finger that bore the royal crest of the House of Dumont. The ring was merely a symbol of a truth that had been with him since the womb. He was Prince Michel Charles Philippe, heir to the throne of Marceau. His father had passed away years ago, and Michel still missed him. Although his mother Queen Anna Catherine had given birth to seven children, she had always been more ruler than mother.

He knew he was envied for his wealth and power. He knew men dreamed of being in his position; of having the final say on any matter in his country.

Michel, however, had experienced the flip side of power, and he was humbled by the scope of his responsibility. For all his power, he couldn't stop the devastation a hurricane had wreaked on Marceau several years ago. Though he held the second-highest position in his country, he couldn't eliminate overnight long-standing social prejudice or ignorance. He couldn't solve all his country's problems in one day.

He might be the wealthiest man in Marceau, and he might be the highest-ranking male in his country, and he might have been trained from an early age to hold himself apart, but he was still just a man.

One

Early in the morning, Prince Michel walked through the hallway toward his office. His mind was divided between the myriad tasks and decisions waiting to greet him and the remnants of his thoughts from last night. He would need to marry soon. A quiet woman of breeding and grace, he thought. A woman who would bring peace and tranquility to the Royal House of Dumont. He continued down the hall, and the click of his heels on the gleaming marble floor did nothing to diminish the volume of loud voices.

"This way, mademoiselle," a man said in a loud, overly enunciated voice. "I will lead you to your quarters."

"Excuse me," a woman nearly shouted. "I'm sorry. What did you say?"

Francois, his son's assistant, was the man. And the woman? Michel took a detour and rounded the corner.

"Mademoiselle Gillian, do you require medication?" Francois asked in exasperation.

"I might," she replied. "I feel like I'm only hearing every other word you're saying."

Michel rounded another corner and caught sight of Francois and a young woman with a mane of curly, wild, red hair. She was dressed in jeans and a T-shirt advertising an American baseball team. Neither garment gave any indication of the shape of her body. Not that he was interested. This woman wouldn't know the meaning of quiet if it banged her on the head.

Francois glanced up and met Michel's gaze. Michel watched panic slice through the man's eyes. Francois immediately gave a quick bow. "Your Highness."

Distracted by the curious but bleary, green-eyed gaze of the woman, Michel gave an absent nod. "Who is our guest?"

"Prince Michel Charles Philipe, may I present Mademoiselle Maggie Gillian? She is here from the United States to tutor Prince Maximillian."

Michel felt an immediate twinge. His son had dyslexia, and learning had become such a chore for him that he avoided all books. Intervention was necessary, so Michel had arranged to import a highly recommended specialist. Mademoiselle Gillian faced the challenge of helping Max overcome his disability.

"Welcome to Marceau, Mademoiselle Gillian. We're pleased you're here to help Maximillian," Michel said.

"Thank you," Maggie shouted back at him. "I'm sorry, but I couldn't hear everything. I didn't catch your name."

Michel shot a quick glance at Francois, who looked slightly ill. "You may call him Your Highness," Francois enunciated so precisely that he nearly spit.

Maggie blinked and gave a vague nod. "Nice to meet you, Your Highness," she said, again too loudly.

Francois winced.

Michel cleared his throat. "Does she have a hearing problem?" he asked in a low voice.

"It's temporary, Your Highness. Apparently her ears were stopped up during the long flight."

Michel relaxed. "Very well. Show her to her quarters before you have to explain her to the guards."

"I'm trying," Francois muttered under his voice, then added, " Your Highness."

Michel left for his office and felt a twist of humor

as the sound of the woman's loud voice echoed down the hallway. Poor Francois.

Eight hours later Maggie awakened to a raging headache. Placing her hands on either side of her face to minimize the pain she was certain she would feel upon moving, she carefully slid from her bed, snatched the headache medicine from her cosmetic bag in the adjoining bathroom, and wrestled with the container. After she freed two pills, she tossed them into her mouth and gulped water directly from the faucet.

She was definitely going to have a *discussion* with her supervisor Carla Winfree when she got near a phone. Burned out from her teaching job at an inner-city public school in Washington, D.C., Maggie had desperately needed a break. Carla Winfree had gotten wind of a secret cushy assignment in the Mediterranean and put Maggie's name in the hat. Maggie had been chosen, but she'd been given very little information about her pupil or the job.

"Such as the fact that I'll be living in a palace," she said and dipped her head under the faucet for another gulp of water. "Such as I'll be teaching a seven-year-old prince. No way he can't be spoiled," she muttered. She splashed her face and wiped it with the hand towel. "Such as I have to deal with a smug, know-it-all pipsqueak by the name of Francois. And a prince, for heaven's sake." A tall, dark, handsome prince who was so stiff he probably had a steel pipe for a backbone. In the short time she'd met Francois and His Highness, she'd gotten the gist that these people were very big on appearances and decorum.

Maggie was not. She took a deep breath and counted to ten. She could deal with attitude. Heaven knows, she'd dealt with attitude from most of the kids she'd taught. But she had a tough time dealing with anyone who put on airs. If there was one thing she didn't like, it was smugness and superiority. Okay, they were two things, but they were related.

"I may not be the right girl for this job." She brushed her teeth and tried not to look at her reflection in the mirror. After a trip halfway round the world, she looked darn frightening.

A knock sounded at her bedroom door, and she eyed it, wishing for a peephole. "Who's there?" she asked.

A brief silence followed, and Maggie could almost feel the exasperation simmering from the other side of the door. "Francois," the irritating man said.

Maggie opened the door and saw Francois with a tray of tea and sandwiches. Her irritation faded slightly. Maybe he wasn't pompous after all. "Please come in," she said.

Relief flooded his face as he entered her room and set down the try. "Your ears are better? *Oui?*"

"Yes, they are. Thank you for the antihistamine and the food. I was starving."

"Not unusual for a trans-Atlantic flight. Your sleep patterns should adjust over the next few days. If you need a sleeping pill, let me know. In the meantime I will brief you on your duties."

Maggie felt the scratchy irritation return. She'd never responded well to an autocratic delivery of orders. "I think I understand my duties. I am to tutor Max because he has dyslexia and he's become so discouraged he no longer tries to learn." She reached for a sandwich and took a bite.

Francois tossed her a suspicious glance. "How did you know of his discouragement?"

"Because I work with these kids every day," she said, and mentally added, *because I've been through the same thing.* "These children bust their butts to keep up, but when they keep failing, they lose heart and hope. It's my job to give a little of that back." She paused. "It must have been tough for the family to come to grips with the fact that Prince Max wasn't perfect."

She took another bite of the sandwich and watched Francois stiffen. "Let me remind you that you are to discuss this with no one. You signed a privacy agreement. The prince's disability is a very delicate matter."

She waved aside his concern. "Well, it shouldn't be. Einstein had a learning disability, too, and he was smarter than anyone walking around this palace.''

Francois inhaled in barely controlled outrage.

Good thing there weren't any flies around or he would have swallowed one, Maggie thought.

''You are not to discuss the prince's disability with anyone besides Prince Michel or me.''

''I won't,'' she assured him. ''But I have to tell you I'm not sure I'm the right girl for this job. I didn't know I would be working with royalty, and I don't have a high tolerance for a lot of unnecessary, prissy protocol. Just in case you can't tell, I'm not a prissy girl.''

''That's quite clear,'' he said in a dry tone as he glanced at her T-shirt and jeans.

Maggie brushed aside the pinch of insult she felt. ''It takes a lot of creativity to get a learning disabled kid up and running, and that's where I keep my focus. I don't have time for unnecessary protocol. My whole goal is to help Prince Max find his joy of learning again, get him confident and reteach him how to read. I'll do whatever it takes to make that happen,'' she said, and silently added, *even though this kid might be so spoiled I can smell him from the other side of the palace.*

Francois gave her a look of guarded respect. ''After you have eaten and freshened up, I will introduce you to Prince Maximillian.''

Truce, Maggie thought. For now.

She finished her sandwich and toiled over what to wear, which was something she never did with her students back in the States. Maggie scowled, then pretended it was Parent Night and dressed in a blue cotton sheath and sandals.

Francois led her to the prince's schoolroom where the boy sat on a sofa watching *102 Dalmatians*.

"Your Highness, I present Mademoiselle Gillian," Francois said.

The boy stood, reluctantly tearing his gaze from the movie. Maggie noticed he was tall for his age. He was dressed in a suit, but his starched shirt was rumpled, and a shirttail hung out of his slacks. His hair was slicked down, but a cowlick on his crown rebelled, reminding her of Dennis the Menace. Maggie's heart softened. Since she'd stood in the shadow of her perfect brother her entire life, Maggie had a deep, abiding compassion for imperfection.

When Francois turned off the movie, she watched the little prince frown, then glance at her with wariness.

"Welcome to Marceau, Mademoiselle Gillian," Prince Maximillian said in a neutral tone.

"Thank you very much, Your Highness. It's a pleasure to meet you. Do you prefer Max or Maximillian?"

The little prince hesitated, and she quickly shot Francois a quelling glance. "Max," the boy finally said.

"Good," she said. "You may either call me Maggie or Miss Gillian."

Max nodded.

"I'm here to help you learn to read and write."

She saw his face immediately shut down. Funny, she thought, prince or pauper, that expression was universal among kids who'd experience too much failure.

"I don't like to read and write."

"I'm not surprised," she said, and wandered around the room eyeing shelves and shelves of unread books.

Max crossed his arms over his chest and looked at her with suspicion. "What do you mean?"

"I mean you've had a rotten experience trying to read and write and you've tried and tried. Trying has made you feel stupid even though you're quite smart."

"How do you know I'm not stupid?" he asked, and her heart broke a little at the doubt in his voice. The glint of defiance in his eyes held a world of pain. She remembered the years in her childhood when she'd felt stupid because she couldn't read.

"Because there are tests that measure learning and intelligence and you score high on the intelligence tests. You have had a problem reading, but I'm here to help you."

Max slid his gaze back to the television. "I would rather watch movies."

She smiled and bent down. "Watching movies can be fun for a while, but you're very smart and you will want to do other things."

He looked at her with a mixture of doubt and curiosity. "Are you American?"

"Yes," Maggie said.

"My father says American women often don't appreciate the importance of royal duty."

Maggie would bet there was a story behind that belief. "That may be true, because we don't have princes and princesses in America."

"My uncle married an American woman."

"What did you think of her?"

"She was nice. She showed me her computer and gave me a piece of chocolate."

Maggie took mental notes. Computers and chocolate. "What's your favorite animal?"

"Dog," Max said without missing a beat. "But I like lions a lot, too."

"Okay," she said, and cataloged the information. "We'll start tomorrow. Good night."

"Good night," Max said, then added, "Mademoiselle Gillian."

Maggie left the room, and Francois guided her down another hall. "Now you will meet with the prince."

Michel set aside thirty minutes to meet with the American tutor, then planned to retire to his quarters with a glass of vintage Burgundy wine and sit in complete and utter silence. It had been one hell of a long day.

A knock sounded at the door. *"Entrez,"* Michel said.

"Your Highness, Prince Michel, may I present Mademoiselle Maggie Gillian."

Michel nodded. "Thank you Francois. You may leave. Please join me, Mademoiselle Gillian," he said, gesturing to the chair across from him.

"Thank you, Your Highness," the woman said and stepped from behind Francois.

Michel blinked at the transformation of the woman he'd met this morning. Although her hair was wild as ever, her green eyes sparked with curiosity and intelligence. Her dress revealed feminine curves and a distracting pair of legs. She moved with a combination of purposefulness and sensuality. She reminded him of a firecracker a palace guard had quickly removed from his hands when he'd been a teenager hell-bent on having fun.

Michel could barely remember the last time he'd genuinely had fun. Between his father's death and the responsibility of the throne that had been his since birth, his life had been unrelentingly serious. Fun was for other people, Michel told himself. He had too many other important matters to manage.

"You have met my son," Michel said.

She nodded. "Yes, and I've read the folder on his

education and test scores. He's very intelligent, but discouraged. Not unusual for children with learning disabilities.''

Michel glanced away. He didn't like the term *learning disability* connected with his son. He still didn't like the idea that there was anything wrong with his son. ''Maximillian is not typical. As you've observed, he is quite intelligent and he will someday rule Marceau.''

She smiled, and her expression warmed him. ''Many parents go through a little grieving stage when they learn their child has a learning difficulty. It's the death of the dream of the perfect child, and it can be painful. That's part of it. But there's another part. I believe kids with learning disabilities are underrated. They view the world differently, and this can be an advantage. I'm sure I don't have to tell you that Einstein had learning problems.''

Michel blinked. He hadn't known. ''Einstein?''

''Oh, yes. His early-childhood teachers told his mother he would never amount to anything. Viewing the world differently can be a good thing. It's my challenge to help Max develop and learn and grow in confidence. I'll tell him that he needs to learn to read a little differently—''

''No—'' Michel began.

''Yes,'' she interrupted, surprising the daylights out of him. No one, save his mother, the queen, interrupted him. ''Prince or ghetto child, I try to be honest and positive with every child I teach," she said firmly. "I'll tell him he can succeed because it's the truth."

"Mademoiselle Gillian," he began.

"Please call me Maggie," she interrupted again. "The formality is unnecessary with me."

Unaccustomed to such a request, Michel paused, then chose to ignore it. He noticed her hands because she laced her fingers and slowly rubbed them back and forth. They were small yet capable looking, her nails unpainted, but something about the flow of her movements struck him as sensual. If she wasn't moving her hands, then she was expressing herself with a slight shrug that made her breasts sway, or she was touching her moist, full mouth. The word to describe her eluded him.

Michel caught himself and, reining in his wandering mind, he returned to the subject at hand. "Maximillian has developed an aversion to books. He has lost all of his confidence."

She nodded. "I can see the aversion to books. He's lost a lot of confidence, but not all. Children are incredibly resilient. A little hope goes a long way." She grew serious. "There is something else I need to discuss with you. I wasn't informed that I would be working in a palace, and I don't know anything about royal protocol. I didn't take any electives on how to curtsy, and—I'll be frank—as far as I'm concerned, it's clutter. I *was* informed that I would have a lot of latitude with this position, to accomplish my goals. If I'm not going to have that latitude, then I'm probably not the woman for this job,'' she said, and slowly stroked her throat.

The way she leaned toward him and kept her gaze on his suggested she was confiding in him, and created an odd sense of intimacy. Michel glanced at her slow-moving finger and his mind's eye traveled down the ivory skin of her neck to her chest. The sheath and whatever she wore beneath dissolved, and he imagined the sight of pale breasts and tight pink nipples. Lower still, he visualized her rib cage and belly button and a downy thatch of hair covering her femininity between her creamy thighs.

He had just mentally undressed his son's tutor, Michel realized and swallowed an oath. He clearly needed a glass of wine and his hour of solitude.

Michel had dealt with everything from foreign affairs to legislation today, but this woman was giving him a headache. ''What do you have planned for Maximillian?''

''I'm going to help him rediscover his passion for learning.''

Her mention of the word passion brushed over his nerve endings, reminding him of passions he'd long denied.

''We're going to do something very important.''

''And what is that, Mademoiselle Gillian?'' he asked.

"Maggie," she corrected with a sensual tilt of her lips. "Max and I are going to have fun."

A few sparse fun-filled memories from his childhood flashed through his mind. Michel wanted the fun for his son, but he also understood the responsibility Maximillian would one day face. "My son will one day rule. Preparing him requires years of training, and there's no way to escape the fact that it's serious business. As an American, you may not appreciate—"

"Oh, Max mentioned you didn't think much of American women."

Michel digested her words and felt a flicker of temper. "Mademoiselle, you've stated that you do not have an appreciation for royal protocol. Is it not considered rude in your country to interrupt when another is speaking?"

He watched her blink, then a look of chagrin crossed her face. She bit her lip. "I apologize. It's hard for me to restrain myself when I feel so passionately about something. You're right."

Michel was accustomed to deference from nearly everyone he met, but her apology and sincere acknowledgment of his point was a breath of fresh air. He nodded. "You'll have a great deal of latitude to accomplish what all of us want for Maximillian, however there are security and protocol factors. It's a fact of life. Francois is an excellent resource for any questions you may have. I'll want a weekly update on Maximillian's progress."

Maggie nodded thoughtfully. "Okay. Just one question please?"

"Yes."

"One of the things I ask the parents of the kids I work with is, do you read with your child?"

Michel felt a haunting sense of loss. "My late wife, Maximillian's mother, sometimes read to him. His nanny has read to him on occasion since then."

Maggie cocked her head to the side. "I'm sorry about your loss. I'm sure you're very busy, but it would help if you can squeeze in some reading every now and then."

"I spend time with my son, but I must delegate some responsibilities to others. That's part of the reason I hired you."

"But I'm a woman, and you're a man."

Silence followed. Her gaze held his, and a basic sensual awareness flashed between them.

Surprise and chagrin crossed her face before she glanced away. She cleared her throat. "This is a modeling issue." She paused when he didn't immediately respond. "Dr. Seuss is highly recommended for children with reading problems."

Michel had a vague recollection of reading a Dr. Seuss book when he was a child. "You want me to read *The Cat in the Hat*," he said, fighting a twinge of impatience. "Mademoiselle, I must teach my son to be a protector, a warrior. I teach him to fence."

She paused a moment. "Your Highness, in your lifetime, how many times have you used a sword to settle your differences or solve a problem?"

"Never," he admitted. "But the sport builds confidence." He held up his hand when she opened her mouth to speak. "I understand what you're saying. Maximillian will use words as a weapon and a bridge far more often than he'll use a sword."

She nodded slowly, and he felt an odd understanding pass between them. He saw a faint glimmer of respect in her eyes at the same time he felt a kick of challenge in his gut. The tutor from America was turning out to be more than he had bargained for.

Two

He wasn't exactly what she'd expected, Maggie thought when the image of Prince Michel skimmed through her mind the next morning. If he had one iota of a sense of humor, he wouldn't be half-bad. She'd found the intelligence and banked emotion in his startling light-blue eyes distracting. His gaze gave hints that there were layers to this man. The notion made her curious. She wondered if he ever let down his guard. She wondered if he could.

He seemed like a man set apart, and something about that bothered her, which was silly, because Prince Michel was none of her concern. Max was. Although she'd struggled with a sliver of intimidation, she'd been determined to treat him just like she treated the parents of her other students.

His sense of honor emanated from him like the heat from the sun. The strength of his character was so rare to Maggie that she was fascinated.

But his confidence had emanated with the same strength as his honor. He seemed almost perfect. Heaven knows, she'd had to put up with enough of that quality from her father and brother. Lifting her hair in a ponytail, she pushed the complex Prince Michel from her thoughts. He was a puzzle best left in someone else's toy box.

She put a map to the palace grounds, a few cue cards and a mirror in a bucket and carried it with her as she headed for Max's personal classroom.

Dressed in perfectly creased slacks, a shirt with the shirttail once again hanging out and a lopsided tie, Max watched the television. Maggie made a mental note for her next conversation with Francois. Max's television time needed to be drastically reduced.

Max glanced up at her, noting her casual shorts and T-shirt with a confused expression.

Spotting the remote, Maggie turned off the TV. "Do you have something special on your schedule today that I don't know about?" she asked.

Max shook his head. "Just school with you," he said, unable to hide his lack of enthusiasm.

"Why are you dressed that way?"

"I always dress this way," he said with just a hint of the same imperial attitude she'd glimpsed in his father.

She smiled. "Well you need to lose the shirt and tie, and change into shorts and tennis shoes, Your Highness."

He glanced at her with a combination of curiosity and suspicion. "What are we going to do?"

She pulled out the map and pointed to an area she'd circled with a red pen. "We're going on a quest to this pond," she told him. "We're going to try to find a frog."

Max's eyes lit up. "A frog?" he echoed with excitement. "I thought we were going to read and write."

"At the right time," she said.

"Bonjour, mademoiselle," Francois said from the doorway. He lifted his eyebrows in disapproval at her attire.

"Good morning, Francois. I was just telling Max to change his clothes. We're going outside today."

Francois immediately stiffened. "Where?"

"Here," she said, pointing to the map.

Francois shook his head. "No."

"Why not? I was told I could use the palace grounds at my discretion," she said.

"That is too far," he said.

"Says who?"

"The palace policy is that Prince Maximillian is

not to wander more than a half mile from the palace itself without an escort.''

She shrugged. "So I'm the escort.''

"An official palace escort,'' he said in a snooty voice that grated on her.

Maggie counted to ten, then bared her teeth in a smile. "Okay. I'll share my sandwich with you. You're welcome to come along.''

"Me!'' Francois exclaimed. "I am not security. I—''

"But you're official, aren't you?''

"Yes, but—''

"And you're definitely from the palace?''

Francois frowned. "Yes, but—''

"And you want Max to get the best possible education, don't you?''

Appearing trapped, Francois narrowed his eyes at her in silence. After a long moment he sighed. "Very well, Mademoiselle Gillian.''

Maggie glanced at Max, who was staring at her, wide-eyed. "Change your clothes, Prince Max. Time's a'wasting.''

As soon as the boy left the room, Francois turned to her. "In the future, it would be best to notify me in advance.''

"Fair,'' she said with a nod. "I'll need someone on standby every day for the next two weeks.''

"But, mademoiselle—''

"Hey, you said you wanted notice.''

Francois gazed at her with an expression of disbelief and disapproval. "But shouldn't you be teaching Prince Maximillian in the classroom?"

"Later." She glanced at Francois's formal dress. "You think you might need to change clothes, too?"

Francois sniffed. "Absolutely not."

"Suit yourself."

A few minutes later Maggie and Max led the way to the pond with Francois unhappily bringing up the rear. "We're going to be looking for tadpoles and frogs," she told Max as they neared the water.

They scoured the area, discussing the various plants and fish they found. When Maggie spotted some tadpoles, she and Max shucked their shoes and waded into the pond to catch them with the bucket. Francois warned her to remain near the edge.

"They're little, but fast swimmers," Max said, staring into the bucket.

"So they won't get gobbled up by the fish," she said with a smile. "We really need our frog now."

She and Max searched until he gave a cry of delight. "I found one!"

"Good job," she said, winding around a cluster of trees. Maggie noticed he didn't pick it up, so she took the frog in her hands and sat down and motioned for Max to join her.

"Okay, what do you notice about this guy compared to the tadpoles?" she asked.

"He's green and he jumps instead of swims, and he's a lot bigger."

The frog wriggled in her hands and made a croaking sound.

Max laughed. "And he's noisier."

"Yes, he is," she said. "Can you make the same sound he does?"

Max was silent for a long moment, then said, "Ribbit, ribbit."

Maggie smiled. "Sounds close to me. The word frog starts with *f*. What does that first sound feel like in your mouth?"

Max made the phonetic sound and gave a blank look.

"Make it again and think about how your teeth and tongue feel." She made the sound with him.

"I feel my teeth on my lips," he said and wrinkled his brow. "And I feel air."

"Excellent. We call that a lip cooler. That's what *f* feels like. Frog starts with *f* and the second letter is *r*. What does *r* feel like?"

Max made the sound. "Buzzy. A car engine in my mouth."

"Very good," she said, delighted and held up the mirror. "Where is your tongue?"

Max made the *r* sound and looked in the mirror. "It's hard to see, but the back of it goes up."

"That's right, and that is why we call an *r* a back

lifter. What about the *ah* sound? How does it feel?" she asked.

He made an *ah*. "Open."

"Yes, and finally *g*," she said. "Where do you feel your tongue?"

"It's touching the roof of my mouth."

"Great," she said. "We call that a tongue scraper. Make that sound one more time, and put your hand on your vocal chords like this," she said, lifting her hand to her own throat.

Max followed her instructions.

"Now just for grins, make a *k* sound, but keep your hand on your vocal chords. And then make the *g* sound again."

He smiled. "When I make the *g* sound I feel it in my throat."

"Very good, now would you like to hold our new friend?"

Max's eyes widened, then he glanced at her cautiously. She saw more than a hint of interest on his face. "Yes," he said, and gingerly extended his hands.

Maggie continued the combination science/phonics lesson until a downpour of rain drenched them. Tossing the tadpoles into the pond, she grabbed Max's hand and they ran back to the palace with Francois.

As they burst through the palace door, she and Max were laughing, but Francois was not.

She glanced up just as three official-looking men rounded the corner with Prince Michel. She watched him pause at the sight of them.

"Oh, Your Highness," Francois said with abject misery as he bowed.

Three of the men gave a nod of deference to Max, then turned their attention to her. Maggie felt the weight of their gazes and was acutely aware of the trickle of water streaming down her back. Fighting an overwhelming feeling of intimidation, she shifted her feet. Her tennis shoes made a squishing sound. She looked like a drowned rat. The three men reminded her of a stuffy version of the Three Stooges. "Uh, hi, Your Highness," she said, and bent her knees slightly. "We got caught in the rain."

"So I see. Gentlemen, this is Mademoiselle Gillian. She is tutoring Maximillian this summer. Lessons outside today?" he asked her with a trace of doubt in his voice.

She felt his gaze take in every drenched detail of her. If she didn't know better, she would have thought his gaze actually lingered on her breasts. But surely that wasn't possible. He was a prince, after all. He probably only had sex for the pure purpose of procreation.

Maggie shook off her distracting thoughts. He'd asked about lessons. "Yes," she said. "Science and phonics."

At that moment the frog jumped out of Max's pocket.

Francois gasped. *"Mon dieu!"*

Maggie raced after the amphibian before he jumped on one of the prissy three men standing next to Prince Michel. "He won't hurt anyone," she said.

Prince Michel's hand closed over the frog just before she reached it. Maggie slowly lifted her gaze to his. "You brought back a visitor," he said.

Maggie's breath stopped in her throat. "Yes, but he's unarmed."

Michel's lips twitched. "Perhaps," he said, then offered the frog to his son. "But I believe he would be happier outside of the palace."

"Yes, Father," Max said, and ducked his head.

Michel paused a moment and ruffled his son's damp hair. "Change your clothes. Remember we have a fencing lesson this afternoon."

Maggie's heart tightened in her chest. It was such a human moment. She heard the combination of firm tenderness in Michel's tone. Michel glanced up at her, and she saw an odd mix of emotion in his eyes. "We shall talk later," he said, and walked away.

As she watched Michel leave, she heard Francois give a heavy sigh. He muttered something in French and shot her a look of pity. Maggie saw the same pity on Max's face.

"Why are you two looking at me that way?" she asked.

"Because my father said he would *talk* with you later," Max said glumly. "And you were such a fun tutor."

"*Were!* I'm still here." She chuckled. "It's not as if he'll send me to the guillotine for getting caught in the rain."

"It's true the guillotine hasn't been used in centuries. It's in the official museum." Francois shook his head. "But I'm afraid Prince Maximillian is correct. You will probably be deported within a day or so. The men accompanying Prince Michel were his advisors, and they looked extremely displeased."

"But the prince didn't seem too upset," she said, surprised at the alarm pinching her stomach. She suddenly wanted the opportunity to complete her work with Max. Although the royal rules and regulations got on her nerves, she wasn't ready to leave.

Francois lifted his chin. "His Highness has been well trained to control his emotions."

A little too well trained, in her opinion. Maggie frowned, then felt a shift in her emotion. "You're saying I'm toast because the advisors didn't like what they saw of me?" She felt a burning sensation flicker through her. "Well, if a little rainwater is going to get those guys' boxers in a twist, then someone needs to sit them down and talk some sense into them."

"Prince Michel's advisors are regarded as the most wise and intelligent men in all of Marceau."

"Then it appears to me that Marceau needs to import more than gasoline and tutors," she said, then turned to Max. "C'mon. If you can get cleaned up quickly, I'll read a book to you."

Max made a face. "I don't like books."

"Bet you'll like this one," she said, taking his hand.

"Bet I won't," he said under his breath as if he'd intended for her not to hear him.

"Bet you will," she retorted with a smile, and squeezed his hand when he looked up at her in surprise.

After cleanup, a Dr. Seuss book and Max's fencing lesson, Maggie was summoned for tea with Prince Michel. When she met him in the parlor, she gave a little dip, then sat in the chair opposite him. "Good afternoon, Your Highness. I appreciate your meeting with me because there is a matter with Max that I think needs immediate attention."

He lifted a dark eyebrow, then waved for the butler to serve the tea. "Thank you," he said after the man poured tea and coffee. "You may be dismissed." He turned to Maggie. "A matter concerning Max," he prompted.

"The television has got to go," she said.

"Max loves his movies."

"I know, but watching television isn't going to help him with his reading."

"Perhaps we could reduce his television time. Maximillian has such limited personal freedom," he said, as if he was well aware of the same limitations in his own life.

"The television shouldn't be in his quarters or his schoolroom. It needs to be inconvenient, at least for a while."

He took a sip of his coffee and regarded her over the edge of his cup. "You are a surprising combination, mademoiselle. You're tough about television but lenient about outdoor lessons."

Maggie had spent the better part of the day wondering if she would be deported, but she told herself she was merely curious. She was not worried. "I was told your advisors would advise you to fire me and that I might very well be leaving within the next day or two."

"But you don't agree," Michel said, surprising her with his perceptiveness.

Maggie looked at him and assessed him for the tenth time. She wondered how long it was going to take her to completely nail his character. "I have this sense that you've been told not to think for yourself for most of your life, and that may have worked for a long while. But you have a very strong mind of your own, and you don't necessarily accept the opinions of your advisors all the time. After all, how old are you? Forty-something?"

Prince Michel blinked, and Maggie had the awful

feeling she'd just stepped over another line. "Thirty-five," he said.

Oops. "Oh, well, I'm sure it's a maturity, responsibility thing. My point is that you strike me as a man who has been around long enough to respect his own opinions."

"My advisors are well informed and grounded in matters of royal tradition, responsibility, training and all issues concerning Marceau."

"I'm sure they are, and I'm sure you're cognizant of the need to not get entrenched."

"You're not afraid of getting *fired,* as you say," Prince Michel said, meeting her gaze dead-on.

Determined to be honest with him, she took a deep breath. "Maybe a little. But I don't really need this job. I'm more concerned about helping Max. We made progress today. If I stay," she told him, "I can't promise we won't get caught in the rain again. Did your advisors hassle the living daylights out of you? Do you ever just tell them to take a chill pill?"

"My sister and most of my four brothers have offered various colorful suggestions to the advisors, but since I work with them daily, I have a different way." He met her gaze as if he were confiding in her. "I tell them I will take their opinions under advisement."

She smiled slowly. "How very restrained and tactful," she said in honest admiration, but would have enjoyed seeing the man in full-fledged anger...or passion.

A knock sounded at the door. Michel gave a slight frown of impatience. *"Entrez,"* he said.

"Pardon me, Your Highness, but Prince Nicholas is here to see you."

Michel's face immediately cleared. "Send him in," he said and stood.

A tall man with shaggy hair, a five-o'clock shadow on his jaw, who was dressed in jeans and a T-shirt strode into the room wearing a crooked smile. He dipped his head, then embraced Michel. "How's the ruling business these days?"

"Busy as always," Michel said. "How is medicine? How long are you home?"

"Until the end of summer. I'm going back to the States for some additional training."

"But while you're here, you will provide consultation for the secretary for health and human services," Michel said.

Nicholas shook his head. "Of course. You're always trying to get me to take a desk job."

"It's natural that I would want the brightest and best for my administration," Michel said.

Nicholas shook his head again, and his expression softened. "You humble me. I'll always be grateful that you helped persuade Mother to allow me to study medicine."

Maggie had the odd feeling that she was observing something very personal. Although she was fascinated by the exchange between the two men, she didn't want to intrude. She stood and began to move toward the door.

"Who's this?" Nicholas asked.

"I should have introduced you," Michel said. "Prince Nicholas is my brother. He is also a medical doctor. This is Mademoiselle Maggie Gillian, Maximillian's summer tutor from the United States."

"It's nice to meet you, Your Highness," she said, uncertain which title she should use, then added, "Doctor."

Nicholas chuckled and lifted her hand to his lips. "Nicholas is fine. Your American accent is refreshing. I suspect the palace protocol is driving you mad."

"Either that or I am driving the protocol police mad," she said, feeling her gaze drawn to Michel.

"Perhaps Francois," Michel conceded.

"And the Three Stooges," she added under her breath.

Nicholas barked with laughter. "You've met the advisors," he said, then turned to Michel. "What a delightful woman. Where did you find her?"

"She's highly recommended in her field," he said. "We should celebrate your arrival tonight."

"This is one of the benefits of leaving the palace. They always throw a party when I return," Nicholas said, turning to Maggie. "You should come."

Reluctance shot through Maggie. It would be a perfect party with perfectly coifed people, and she would feel so out of place. "Oh, thank you, but I don't think so."

"Yes," Prince Michel said, surprising the daylights out of her. "You must come."

"But isn't there some rule about employees mixing with the royals?"

"Are you refusing my invitation?" Prince Michel asked her in the same silky voice she suspected he used when he told his advisors he would take their opinions under advisement.

She could almost have sworn she saw a flare of sexual challenge in his eyes. Her heart raced. Not possible, she told herself. She cleared her throat. "I get the impression it's a big no-no to refuse Your Highness's invitation."

"That would be correct," Prince Michel said.

She held her breath, certain the electricity she felt zinging between Michel and her was her imagination. "Then I guess that means I'm coming to a party tonight. Does this also mean I'm still employed as Max's tutor?"

"Of course," Michel said.

"Even though your wise counsel might have suggested otherwise," she said, unable to resist the slight taunt.

"The advisors offer advice. I make decisions," Michel said.

"There's a story here," Nicholas said, glancing from Maggie to Michel. "I can't wait to hear it."

"Later," Michel said, glancing at his watch. "I have an appointment with the prime minister in a few minutes. You can rest and decide if you want to demonstrate your rebellion with your hair and wannabe beard," he said to his brother with a wry grin. "Mother's out of the country, so it may not be as much fun for you."

Nicholas gave a mock sigh. "An advantage to being born third instead of first is that the only person who nags me when I don't shave is my mother. Michel is required to be perfect."

"Don't let Nicholas mislead you. He's no slouch. His academic performance has been stellar. He just likes to play the role of the unprince," Michel said, his pride in his brother obvious and appealing. "If I ever get a day off, I may skip shaving, too."

"I won't hold my breath," Nicholas said with a mix of humor and respect. "My brother is what you Americans call a type-A overachiever."

Michel rolled his eyes. "As enjoyable as this is, I must leave for my meeting. I'll see you both tonight," he said, then left the room.

"A man in demand," Nicholas mused. "He has been since he was born." He turned his curious gaze on Maggie. "You've impressed him."

Maggie made a face. "I think *disrupted* would be a more accurate description."

"A little disruption is good for him," Nicholas said. "What do you think of my brother?"

"I don't know him very well. I don't know him at all, really."

"But you have an opinion," Nicholas prodded.

"My opinion is just forming," she hedged, reluctant to share her thoughts with anyone.

"With the exception of my mother and sister, my brother is accustomed to women who agree with every breath he takes. I suspect you're not so agreeable."

"You suspect correctly," she said. Finding Michel's brother entirely too perceptive, she decided to leave. "It's a pleasure to have met you, Your Highness—Doctor. Please excuse me while I make the futile search for something appropriate to wear to your party tonight." She wondered if there was a way she could skip the event.

"You must attend," Nicholas reminded her, as if he could read her mind.

"Yes, I know," she muttered, still hoping for a way out. "Orders from His—" *High and Mightiness,* she added for her own benefit. "Orders from The Man. I'll see you tonight," she said, and headed for her room, her mind filled with thoughts of Michel.

So there was heart and determination behind the perfect facade. She felt herself surprisingly drawn to Michel. It was as if the lens through which she viewed him cleared a little more and she saw him in a different light. Another layer revealed. Her respect and fascination grew, as did her questions. As a teacher, Maggie knew the power of curiosity. She was also mature enough, however, to know that curiosity about a man could lead a woman down a treacherous path.

But the more she learned about Michel, the more she wanted to know.

Three

She laughed a little too loudly. Her dress was unsuitably casual. Her hair was as impertinent as her personality.

But every man in the room kept looking at her.

Michel knew he was no exception.

Irritated, he tried to focus on the lovely, soft-spoken widowed countess who had been fawning over him all evening. He nodded as she continued to praise the wine selection. Michel considered telling her he'd had no part in that decision, but he refrained. Barely.

His sister-in-law caught his eye and took pity on him. Auguste's wife, Anjolie, walked toward him and smiled at the countess. "We're delighted you could attend this evening, Countess Brevard. The royal palace has a beautiful selection of Renoir paintings in one of the parlors. I'd love to show you."

"Take a breather," Anjolie murmured for his ears only.

Michel nodded his silent gratitude and immediately headed for the balcony. The scent of flowers was sweet in the humid night air, the string quartet played a soothing refrain, and the lights from the cottages throughout the countryside glittered like a thousand candles.

He inhaled deeply. Before he had time to exhale, however, his moment of respite was invaded by a swirl of red hair and a groan as Maggie ducked into the balcony and leaned against the wall.

Michel watched her for a long moment before he spoke. Her skin glimmered in the moonlight, her lips shiny, her eyelids closing out the world.

"You don't like the party?" he ventured.

Her eyes flashed open in surprise. "Oh! I thought I was alone."

He lifted an eyebrow. "So did I."

"Sorry. I can look for a closet."

Unable to restrain a smile, he shook his head. "No. You can stay. But you didn't answer my question. You don't like our party?"

She met his gaze in the dark. "Do you want me to be tactful or truthful?"

"Truthful," he said immediately. He couldn't explain it, but he craved her particular brand of honesty.

"It's a little stiff. It needs something. Motown or Lenny Kravitz."

"A boombox blaring a remake of 'American Woman,'" he said, certain his ancestors would turn back flips in their graves.

She looked at him in surprise. "*You've* heard of Lenny Kravitz?"

Irritated, he recalled how she'd assessed his age as older. He shouldn't give a damn she viewed him that way, but he did. "You expected me to be familiar only with dead classical composers?"

She winced. "Well, I haven't heard those strings try any hip-hop. I guess I just thought the music would reflect your personality."

"And that is?" he asked, his tone clipped, to his own ears.

She hesitated. "I don't really know you well enough to judge."

"Exactly," he said.

"But if I had to say," she continued, "I would describe you as restrained, so I would expect your taste in music might reflect that quality." She studied him for a moment. "Do you ever yell?"

He felt like yelling *right now*. "The problem with

a man in my position yelling is the chain effect it causes. For example, if I had a screaming match with you right now, the guards would rush out here and haul you off to interrogate you. Even though you would be cleared of any hypothetical charges, you would be regarded with suspicion during the rest of your stay in Marceau.''

She looked at him with a combination of empathy and sympathy.

Irritation nicked through him again. "I don't need your sympathy," he said.

Her eyes widened as if she were surprised he'd read her so easily. She met his gaze, then walked closer to him and shook her head. "How can I not feel sorry for you? Your position can't help but make you incredibly lonely and isolated.''

"I'm surrounded by people every day.''

"Surrounded by people with whom you must measure every word, every gesture. Is there anyone you can trust enough to yell or cry or joke with?''

"I can joke with my sister and brothers," he said, then honesty forced him to add, "at times.''

She shrugged. "Call me crazy, but it looks to me as if you work damn hard for this country. I think you deserve to have someone looking out for your good.''

"I have many servants who make sure I am fed what pleases me and take care of my clothing. I have a palace doctor at my disposal.''

She shook her head and extended her hand as if she were going to touch him. At the last moment she pulled back as if she'd thought better of the action. Michel felt an odd sense of loss.

"I don't think you're getting it," she said. "Who worries about your personal happiness?"

Her question silenced him, echoing inside him. His happiness. What a novel concept. What an impossible concept. He brushed it aside. "My happiness isn't the top priority."

"Well it should be for somebody," she said. She hesitated a moment, then lifted her lips in a slow grin. "With your personal happiness in mind, I think I'll give you a few moments' peace. Excuse me," she said, and left him with the terrible sense that she had just found and opened his Pandora's box.

Later that night Michel couldn't sleep. He wandered the length of his bedchamber, thinking about what Maggie had said. The notion of his happiness had always been a forbidden area of thought for him, and he had avoided asking himself futile what-if questions. Sighing, he glanced outside a window and caught a flash of white in the courtyard. Narrowing his eyes, he took a closer look.

A woman dressed in a short nightgown wandered barefoot through the grass. His lips twitched. Maggie. He wondered if she'd remembered to prop the door to the palace open. If not, she was stuck and would have to pound on the door and wake up the guards.

Michel glanced at his phone. It would be easy to call a guard to let her in. He could punch the three-number extension, issue a one-sentence order and return to…ruminating and insomnia. He swore at the prospect.

Maggie sat down on the stone love seat and inhaled a breath of fresh air. She couldn't bear one more minute inside the palace. The walls felt as if they were closing in on her. When she'd laid down on her bed, she'd thought about Max and Michel. She wasn't worried about Max learning to compensate for his dyslexia. He was already responding to his lessons. She couldn't, however, help worrying about his future. He would one day rule, but would he ever be happy? Not if he followed in his father's footsteps. She frowned. What a suffocating life Prince Michel led. Someone should fix it, she thought, although she had no idea how. And, of course, it shouldn't be up to her to fix it; it was none of her business.

Her only concern was supposed to be Max's academics, but she would have to be a piece of wood not to respond to Max's thirst for adventure. Even though Prince Michel appeared disgustingly perfect, she thought and made a face, his sense of honor got to her.

Groaning, she stood, restlessly stomping over the grass. She'd come outside to *stop* thinking about Max and Michel. Mentally slamming the door on the two princes, she focused on the scent of the flowers.

"The next time you take an evening stroll, you might want to leave the door open," a voice said from behind her.

Startled, Maggie whirled around to see Prince Michel's shadow in the darkness. Her heart hammered in her chest. "Excuse me?"

He walked toward her, wearing a pair of lounging pants and an open shirt, looking moody and masculine in the moonlight. "The palace doors are locked every night at 9:00 p.m. You would have a tough time getting back in."

Off-balance, she gave an uncertain laugh. "I, uh, guess this wouldn't be a great time to ring the royal doorbell, huh?" She glanced at the door, which was now propped open, then back at Michel. She tried not to stare at his muscular chest. "Thank you for rescuing me."

He gave a slight dip of his head. "My pleasure."

An uncomfortable moment of silence passed. She folded her hands together in front of her. "I'm not ready to go in yet," she said.

"Neither am I," he said.

Was he was looking at her the way a man would look at a woman if he was interested? Her heart raced. That couldn't be, she told herself. It must have been a trick of the moonlight. She tore her gaze from his and wandered to a nearby tree. She touched the smooth, cool bark and tried to clear her head.

"Shouldn't you be sleeping?" she asked. "Don't you have at least three appointments tomorrow?"

"Six," he said, walking toward her. "I'll trade the fresh air for a few moments of sleep."

Her curiosity sprang up like a weed, and she glanced at him. "Do you ever sleep in?"

He paused, then laughed. "I can't remember the last time I slept late. Maybe college, after I stayed too long at a party. Feels like forever," he said, staring into the distance.

A forbidden urge to touch him sprang out of nowhere. She'd wanted to several times. Although he was clearly strong, his isolation bothered her. "Where did you go to college?"

"Oxford."

"How many wild oats did you sow there?"

He lifted his lips in a dangerous smile. "Not as many as I'd wanted to sow. And you?"

Surprise rushed through her. "Me? Wild oats?" She shook her head. "I didn't have time. I was too busy trying to keep my head above water with my studies."

He frowned, shaking his head. "Your résumé said you graduated cum laude."

"With a lot of thank-you, 'laude,' mixed in," she

muttered. "One of the reasons I wanted to teach kids with dyslexia was because I'm dyslexic."

His eyes widened and he arched his eyebrows. "Is that so?"

"Yep, it's not on my résumé, but the experience of being dyslexic probably contributes to my effectiveness with my students as much as my education does. I know what it feels like."

"What did it feel like?" he asked in a low voice.

"Horrible," she said. "I hated going to school. I would break out in a sweat whenever the teacher asked me to read. I spent a lot of time trying to hide my problems. I felt so stupid, and my brother was a perfect student. My parents didn't understand why I wasn't perfect, too."

"What changed things for you?"

"I had a teacher who was very persistent. She would stay after school to work with me. She told me I was smart. She believed in me, and she made it okay for me to be different."

"She gave you power," he concluded, perceptive again.

"Yes, she did," she said, pleased that he understood.

"And that's what you hope to give to Maximillian."

"That's what I'll help Max find in himself." She met his gaze, and his mere presence unsettled her. His unrelenting aura of strength got to her. Maggie was accustomed to the cubic zirconian version of strength, a superficial display of physical or financial muscle. Heaven knew, she'd had to put a brave face on a few bad situations herself. But she knew that when she looked at Michel, she was looking at the Hope diamond of strength—the real thing—and she was pretty darn sure Michel's power went deeper than his bones.

"You have always known you had power, haven't you?" she asked, her voice sounding husky to her own ears.

He nodded. "Always known it. But I haven't always understood it. That may take a lifetime."

She saw undercurrents of duty and curiosity in his light eyes, and the combination was incredibly appealing to her. *Who was she fooling?* The combination was sexy to her. It surprised the heck out of her.

"What are you thinking at this very moment?" he asked, his gaze searching hers as he moved closer. She instinctively backed against the tree.

A sliver of alarm shot through her, and she bit her lip. "Umm," she began, knowing she definitely needed to hedge, but her mind was too clouded. She sucked in a quick breath of air and inhaled his clean, masculine scent.

He lifted his hand to touch a strand of her hair. "Tell me," he ordered.

He spoke the words with such authority that she

felt compelled to do as he said. But she stopped herself. "Not in a million years," she whispered.

He went completely still. "Pardon?"

If you dare, she read in his gaze. She cleared her throat. "I'd prefer not to discuss what I'm thinking."

"I prefer you tell me," he said, again touching her hair.

Maggie was having a tough time breathing. "But it's my brain, so in this one situation, you don't rule. I do."

He paused a long moment. "In another time I could have had you thrown in the dungeon for defying me."

"You wouldn't have," she said, "even in another time."

He lifted an eyebrow. "I wouldn't?"

"You would have been too creative to use the dungeon routine. There are more effective ways of getting someone to talk."

His lips tilted in a sexy half-smile. "Such as?"

"I don't know. Take away my CDs, my baseball games. Promise me chocolate-dipped strawberries."

"The passions of Maggie Gillian," he said.

"Some of them," she said with a shrug, sinking into his light-blue gaze.

He gave her hair a gentle tug to get her attention. He clearly didn't know he'd never lost it. "For a moment," he said, in a voice like velvet, "you looked at me as a man, not a prince."

Her chest squeezed tight with an emotion she couldn't name. Closing her eyes, she tried to take a deep breath to dispel it.

"Didn't you?" he asked.

He only touched a single strand of her hair, but her awareness of him suffused her. She swallowed. "What if I did?" she retorted, but the breathy sound in her voice diminished the punch of her words.

"Open your eyes," he told her.

She automatically did as he commanded, then frowned. "You give a lot of orders."

"Downside of the job," he said, not taking his gaze from hers. "I want to kiss you."

Before she could do more than stare in surprise, he slid his hand around the nape of her neck and took her mouth with his.

Her mind still frozen, she felt instinct take over. Her lips parted beneath the gentle pressure of his, and she felt him rub his mouth against hers in a slow, seductively exploring motion. She sensed this was a man who knew how to seduce a woman. A dozen protests sprang up in her mind, but the rapid hammering of her heart drowned them out.

His hard chest brushed her breasts, tempting, teasing, and she felt her nipples harden. She grasped for a millimeter of sanity. The edge of his tongue slid over her upper lip with just the right amount of pressure to make her curious what he would do next.

Pleasure taunted her. *It's just a kiss,* she told herself.

But he's a prince.

Not at this moment.

His low sound of approval disarmed her. His heat warmed, his mouth aroused. He kissed her as if she were a delicacy and he wanted to savor her. He slid his tongue over her tender inner bottom lip in an invitation she couldn't refuse. She caressed him in return, cupping her tongue around his, drawing him more deeply into her mouth.

The kiss went on, evolving into an erotic simulation of how his body would take hers, how her body would receive his. Maggie felt her nether regions grow swollen.

She heard a sensual moan of need slide through the thick air, and a full moment passed before she realized she'd made the sound. She wanted— Another moan escaped. She needed air. She needed sanity.

Maggie dragged her mouth from his and lowered her head to his chin. "Oh, wow. You're not supposed to kiss—" she drew a long breath "—like that."

He tangled his fingers in the back of her hair and skimmed his lips over her forehead. "How am I supposed to kiss?"

She bit her lip at the desire still clamoring through her. "I dunno. Just not like that."

"How?" he demanded.

She shook her head and willed her brain to work. "Less," she began, but her thoughts were still scrambled. "More—"

He gave a gentle tug on her hair. "More what?"

She made a sound of frustration. "More princely," she said, and met his gaze defiantly.

Amusement warred with arousal in his eyes. "What is *princely?*"

"More restrained," she said, and tugged his hand away from her. This was one man with whom she definitely needed all her spark plugs firing correctly.

"Less sexy," she said firmly, and waved her hand at him. "You royal types only have sex for the purpose of procreation. You're not supposed to be sexy."

Michel gave a roar of laughter that sent a ripple through Maggie. The sound was so unrestrained, full of passion.

He shook his head, and the look in his eyes sent a thrill licking over her nerve endings. "Teacher, you have a lot to learn about royals, a lot more than protocol."

Four

You have a lot to learn about royals, a lot more than protocol.

Prince Michel's words vibrated inside her, every other moment, and a steamy image of him permeated her mind. She mentally scowled. What Mr. High-and-Mighty didn't understand was that understanding princes was *not* required course work for Maggie. It was completely optional, and if she had half a brain, which she did, then she would opt out. And she simply would never think about the *omigod* way he'd kissed her last night.

Uh-huh, her contrary mind said in disbelief.

Maggie scowled again, and returned her attention

to Max. They'd just completed a lesson and she'd read a book by Dr. Seuss to him. The little prince gave a heavy sigh and looked longingly at the rain-splattered window, then the television.

"I want to watch a movie," he said.

"Another time," she said, standing and looking around the room. "Let's play a board game. What do you like?"

"Chess," he said, surprising her.

"Chess?" she echoed.

He nodded. "All the Dumont men play chess. It's tradition."

"What about the Dumont women?"

He shrugged. "I don't know. My cousins are girls, and they don't play."

His attitude ruffled her feminist side. "If it's a family tradition, then there's no reason the Dumont women can't learn."

"Do you know how to play?" he asked with a crafty expression on his face.

"No," she said. "But—"

"We can watch television."

"—but I can learn. You can teach me."

His eyes widened in surprise. "Me?"

"Why not?"

"You're the teacher."

"Yes, and I'm here to help you with your reading. But you're a very smart boy, and there are things I

can learn from you, too," she said. "Like chess."
She clapped her hands. "So let's get started."

A hint of pride lifted his chin as he rose from the
table. "I'll get my set."

After a few moments he returned and set up the
board. "These are the pawns," he said pointing to
the smallest playing pieces. "You can only move
them forward one space at a time, except the first
time when you can move them two spaces. And you
can move them diagonally to take out another piece.
The rooks look like castle towers and they move
forward, backward and sideways any number of
spaces. But they can't move diagonally. The knights
look like horses and they move in an *L* shape only.
Like two spaces up and one space over. The bishops
look like pawns, only they're taller and they move
only diagonally any number of spaces...."

Maggie's head began to swim. "Wait a minute.
Why did I think this game was just a glorified form
of checkers? Are there any more?"

"Just the queen and the king," Max said, and
lifted his lips in a smile reminiscent of his father.
"Don't worry. I'll let you go first."

Prince Michel checked his watch and frowned.
Max was late for his fencing lesson, and Max was
never late. Michel could have sent a palace assistant
to collect his son, but he thought better of it. He

would check Max's room himself. Who knows? He might run into Max's witchy teacher.

Michel checked Max's bedroom, then walked toward Max's classroom.

A shriek cut through the air. "My queen! You thief! You took my queen!"

Confused, Michel threw open the door. Maggie was pounding the table while Max gleefully held a chess piece in his hand. Michel couldn't remember seeing his son so animated. A warm feeling suffused him, invading his chest. He locked the moment in his mind, wanting more happy moments for his son.

Max glanced up, and his smile fell. His eyes widened and he gasped. He stood. "Oh, Father, I forgot my fencing lesson," he said, clearly appalled.

Michel took in the sight of half-eaten sandwiches and the expression on Maggie's face. She also stood. "It's my fault, Your Highness. I asked Max to teach me to play chess, and it appears I'm a slow learner," she said dryly.

"Oh, no," Max said. "You lasted much longer during this game. Besides, just because I got your queen doesn't mean I've won. You still have your king."

"I appreciate your kindness, Max, but you and I both know the king isn't worth squat without the queen." She turned back to Michel. "Your son cleaned my clock."

Michel watched Max beam and felt a rush of gratitude toward Maggie. His gaze dipped to her mouth and he remembered how she'd tasted. "It looks like you two have been at it for a while. Just curious. How many games have you played?"

"Four," Max said. "She was terrible during the first two, but she really was getting better during this last one."

"He's being kind again," Maggie said. "Look at all my pieces he's taken."

Michel's lips twitched with humor. "Good job, Max," he said. "We still have time for a short lesson. Get changed and meet me in the gym."

Max zoomed out of the room, and Michel turned to Maggie. "Thank you," he said.

She lifted her shoulders as if she didn't understand. "For what?"

"For playing chess with Max."

She smiled. "Your son is cool," she said. "A little sexist at times, but I imagine that's not his fault."

Michel raised his eyebrows. "Sexist?"

She nodded. "Oh, yes. He told me the Dumont *men* learn to play chess. He also said the Dumont *men* fence. I guess I'll have to ask him for fencing lessons next."

"Absolutely not," Michel said, feeling the slightest twinge of envy toward his son. God help him, that was ridiculous.

"Why not?"

"Maximillian isn't experienced enough to teach you to fence. If you learn to fence, you'll learn from me."

"Why does that sound like a royal decree?"

"Because you're American and you're not accustomed to being around a man who speaks with authority."

"Are you sure it doesn't have more to do with being bossy?"

"The only other person who has come close to suggesting I was bossy was my sister, Michelina."

"Isn't that interesting?" she murmured with a mock-innocent expression. "And she's not American, is she? She's just female. I wonder what that says."

Her defiance aroused the hell out of him. He wondered if she had any clue. Michel moved toward her. "I find your mouth exasperating."

She pressed her lips together tightly, an unsuccessful attempt at looking prim. Maggie couldn't be prim in a million years. Her generous mouth was made for pleasure. Her green gaze grew wary as if she were remembering the hot kiss they'd shared. "Are you sure you don't mean my opinions are exasperating?"

"Those, too," he said. "But your mouth is also—" he slowly lifted his gaze from her lips "—distracting.

"Really? Most people say that about my hair."

She glanced at her watch. "Don't let me keep you from the fencing lesson."

A tinge of irritation scraped through him. "Maximillian will need to put on additional equipment in the gym. Are you dismissing me?"

Her eyes widened, and she licked her lips nervously. "Oh, no," she said in an unconvincing voice. "I just know you're a busy man and your schedule is probably crammed."

"But you've told me I should make time for my own enjoyment."

"Yes," she agreed with a nod. "But not with me."

He dipped his head for further explanation and slowly backed her against the wall.

She winced as if she realized she was being backed against the wall verbally as well as physically. "I mean, I'm sure there are lots of other people you could enjoy more than me."

He wrapped his finger around one of her springy curls. "Are you saying you didn't like the way I kissed you last night?"

She bit her lip, and her gaze skittered away from his. "I, uh—" she cleared her throat "—I think I prefer to plead the fifth."

"We don't have the fifth in Marceau," he said.

"We already discussed this last night," she said. "I don't see why—"

"Exactly," he said in agreement, and took her

mouth with his. He tasted her gasp and dipped his tongue across the seam of her lips. Two seconds passed before she opened her mouth to his and tasted his tongue with hers. He felt the dark rush of arousal at her response to him. Her velvet, curious stroke made his blood rush through his veins, pooling in his crotch. It was so easy to imagine her sensual mouth on his naked skin, skimming over his abdomen and lower, where he grew hard with wanting. He felt more alive, more human than he could ever remember. Michel made a decision.

"Come to my room tonight," he said.

She gave a soft panicked moan. "Oh, no. That's not a good idea."

"Why not?"

"Because we don't know each other well enough."

"I know enough," he said. "I can take care of you."

Her eyes dark with arousal, she shivered slightly. "I don't know enough about you," she said, and pulled back. She laced her fingers together, then unlaced them as she began to pace. "I didn't come to Marceau to become your mistress. I'm really not mistress material," she told him.

"You'd rather be married," he said, knowing that prospect was impossible.

She looked at him in alarm. "Oh, Lord, no. There

are too many things I want to do, and a husband would really cramp my style.''

"Then you would be happy being my mistress," he said.

She wrinkled her brow. "I'm happy being single and pursuing my interests.''

"And I am your interest," he said.

She shot him a look of consternation. "Your ego is bigger than this palace.''

"Am I incorrect? Are you interested in me?" he challenged.

She turned silent. "No. You're not incorrect. You are interesting to me. That doesn't mean I should do anything about it.''

"But you will."

She lifted her chin. "Another order?"

"No," he said, because he felt a sense of fate about this woman. He would know her. He would take her. "Fact. Now, I must leave for Maximillian's lesson. *Au revoir.*''

Maggie gaped after him. *"Au revoir,"* she mocked, not unlike one of her students. She gave a heavy sigh, blowing her hair out of her face.

What was she getting herself into?

Nothing, she told herself firmly. She could handle Max, and Max was the real reason she was here in Marceau, not his fascinating, surprisingly sexy father.

She wandered around Max's classroom, trailing her fingers over the solid wood furniture. She couldn't deny that she was drawn to Michel, but as far as Maggie was concerned, the man had danger signs flashing all around him. Although she was more adventurous than the average bear, she believed in being somewhat sensible. For example, even she knew and accepted the fact that there were some neighborhoods in Washington to avoid at night.

But when Michel looked at her with undivided attention, when he kissed her, her heart jumped. It sounded hokey, but when they talked something happened in the air between them and around them.

Maggie nibbled her index fingernail. And he'd suggested she become his mistress. She wrinkled her nose. The notion assaulted every independent fiber of her being. Besides that, it felt, well, icky.

She'd never taken much time for romance. There'd always been more important things to do, and she'd fought so hard to come out from behind the shadow of her brother and dominating father that she'd never wanted to put herself in such a position again.

And she didn't want to get involved now, she told herself firmly. At the same moment she couldn't help thinking what a powerful combination of a man Michel was. She wondered if she would ever meet a man like him again. She wondered if she truly wanted to let the opportunity to know this extraordinary man, his heart, mind and body slip through her fingers.

"Mademoiselle, this is the third time you have taken Prince Maximillian for one of your field trips," Francois said the following day as he mopped his brow with a handkerchief. "Isn't this excessive?"

"It's a reward," Maggie told him. "He has shown improvement already, and he worked hard this morning. Right, Max?" she said to the boy skipping slightly ahead.

He nodded as he swung the bucket. "You should have worn shorts, sir."

"Maybe you could roll up your pants," she suggested.

Francois looked down his nose at her. "I think not," he said. "And you should know Prince Michel is aware of all your activities. He asks for an accounting every day."

Maggie came to a dead stop. "Are you saying he's asked you to watch me?" she asked.

Francois seemed to grasp the slight pique in her tone. "Well, not in so many words."

"In exactly what words, then?"

She felt Max come to her side and glanced down at him. He looked at her and Francois and pulled at her hand. "My father does the same with me," Max said as if he wanted to placate her. "He doesn't have time to be with me all day every day, but he still wants to know about me every day. He always says if anything happens and he knows about it, then he can take care of me better."

Sometimes Max's sensitivity amazed her. "Take care of you how?"

Max shifted from one foot to the other. "The advisors and sometimes, Grandmother, the queen, can be, well, fussy."

"Prince Michel is quite protective," Francois said with pride.

"But I don't really need protecting," Maggie said.

Francois hesitated. "The advisors have opinions about almost everything," he said in a hushed voice as if he feared the butterflies fluttering nearby might repeat his words.

Realization hit her. "Oh, the advisors still don't like me."

"It's not so much a matter of liking as approving," Francois said, tugging at his collar, clearly uncomfortable with the discussion.

"Hmm," she said shortly with a sniff, then allowed Max to pull her forward. "They'll approve the results."

"That is what Prince Michel says," Francois said.

"And what Prince Michel says, goes," Maggie

said, remembering his assertion that they would be lovers.

"As it should," Francois said.

She could disagree, but she bit her lip and focused on helping Max enjoy the beautiful day. They caught more tadpoles and waded at the water's edge. Francois fussed if they waded more than a few feet from the edge of the pond. Ignoring him, Maggie talked about the life cycles of tadpoles and frogs. They nibbled on sandwiches and tossed a few crumbs to the fishes.

Max spotted a turtle on a rock farther out in the pond, and he was so excited Maggie would have thought he'd found the Holy Grail. Unable to resist the longing in his eyes, she waded out to the rock, getting wet up to her waist. She grabbed the turtle and returned. On the way, she stepped on something sharp.

"Ouch!"

"What is it?" Francois asked. "Did something bite you?"

"No, I stepped on something," she said, feeling her foot burn with pain.

"Are you okay?" Max asked. "Are you bleeding?"

The worried expression on his face tugged at her heart. "I'm sure it's just a scrape," she said, even though it hurt like the dickens. "Here, put the turtle in the bucket. You get to name him, but his name needs to start with a *T*."

"We're not taking that...that amphibian back to the palace," Francois said in an appalled voice.

"Reptile," she corrected. "We have to. We just got him and I think I could use a Band-Aid."

Max looked at her foot as she walked out of the pond. "You're bleeding," he said, and bit his lip.

"I'll be okay," she assured him. "I just need a Band-Aid." She sneaked a glance at the bottom of her foot and swallowed a wince at the dirty gash.

Francois pursed his lips, then opened his mouth, but Maggie cut him off with a shake of her head. "Sorry, but I think we need to get back. Let me put on my shoes."

During the walk to the palace, she helped Max think of names for the turtle. By the time they arrived, Maggie was grinding her teeth at the pain. "You go clean up," Maggie told Max. "And I'll do the same."

"But what about your foot?" he asked.

"I'll take care of it. You go on ahead. Okay?"

As soon as he disappeared down the hall, she turned to Francois. "Please get me a first aid kit."

"There's always a doctor on call for the palace."

"Not necessary," she said. "I'm going to take a shower. Please leave the kit on my bed."

She entered her room, stripped, turned the shower on hot and bit down on a washcloth while she cleaned her wound. Pulling on a big, fluffy terry cloth robe, she sat on the closed commode and looked at her foot. "A butterfly bandage," she murmured without much hope.

Sighing, she stood and opened the bathroom door. Prince Michel and Nicholas stood waiting for her. Her heart caught at the intense expression in Michel's gaze.

"We're here to see the foot," Nicholas said.

"Francois is such a busybody," she muttered, hopping forward. Before she could take a second hop, Michel scooped her up in his arms and carried her to her bed.

Nicholas immediately took her foot in his hands and made a clucking sound. "Stitches," he said.

"I was hoping a butterfly bandage," she began.

He shook his head. "Stitches and a tetanus shot."

"You're a regular messenger of joy," she said, and watched him pull a needle and sutures from his black bag.

"You shouldn't be careless with yourself," Michel admonished.

"I wasn't careless," she said. "Just a little adventurous. I had to get Tex."

"Tex?" Michel echoed.

"I'm surprised Francois didn't blab that part, too. Tex, the turtle, was on a rock out in the pond."

Nicholas chuckled and put a fat towel beneath her foot. "Something tells me Tex is no longer in the pond. Antibacterial antiseptic,'' he said, and spilled cool liquid from a bottle. ''Cream for numbing,'' he said. ''I'll stick you next.''

''You waded into the pond for a damn turtle,'' Michel said.

''Max wanted it,'' she said. She felt the prick of the needle and winced.

''He could have lived without it,'' Michel said.

''It's not like it was a pony. It was just a turtle. It wouldn't have been that big a deal if I hadn't cut my foot. Don't you need to be meeting with some sort of ambassador or making legislation or something?''

''I can handle my schedule,'' he said in a too-soft voice of warning.

Despite her bravado, she felt a shiver of apprehension. She clamped her mouth shut while Nicholas worked on her foot. Michel paced beside her bed. The young doctor smiled gently when he finished, gave her a few instructions and squeezed her shoulder before he left.

Michel shoved his hands in his pockets and sighed impatiently. ''You shouldn't be so careless.''

''I told you I wasn't careless,'' she protested. The tension emanating from him made her stomach knot.

He sat down on the bed beside her and took her hand in his.

Maggie glanced down at the way his large, strong hand enveloped hers. The protective gesture tugged at something deep inside her. "I'm going to be okay," she said, meeting his gaze. "It's not as if I was attacked by a shark."

Michel groaned. "God forbid." He shook his head. "My son doesn't like to see you hurt."

Maggie's heart softened. "I know."

"Neither do I," Michel said, his gaze completely focused on her.

There was something beyond desire in his eyes. Tenderness. She saw it, and the effect slipped past her defenses like smoke through a keyhole.

Five

Michel listened to Nicholas's stories of his recent trip to America while the two brothers shared breakfast in Michel's office. One of his assistants interrupted with an expression of regret.

"Monsieur Faus wishes to see you briefly, sir."

Monsieur Faus was his least favorite advisor. As soon as Michel formally took the throne, he planned to retire Faus with honors. "After Nicholas and I finish breakfast," Michel told him.

The assistant gave a hesitant nod. "Yes, Your Highness. Monsieur Faus preferred to have a private word with you before the general meeting with the other advisors."

Michel frowned. Faus was going to make a fuss about something. He wondered what. "I'm sure he said it was an issue of grave concern."

The assistant nodded and gave a slight grimace. "Yes, sir."

"I don't mind. We're almost finished," Nicholas said. "I haven't had the pleasure of talking with Fausy in years. I'm surprised he's still around."

Michel resisted the urge to agree, then tossed his napkin on the table and nodded at the assistant. "Tell him I have five minutes."

Faus, a tall, self-important man with bulging eyes, was admitted to the office and gave a slight bow. "Your Highnesses."

Nicholas nodded. "Good morning."

Faus turned back to Michel. "I have an issue of grave concern to our country."

"Does this issue concern military, crime or famine?" Michel asked.

"No. It involves our future ruler, your son."

Michel tamped down the scratchy irritation he felt at the back of his neck.

"It has come to my attention that his American—" he said the word with disdain "—tutor endangered him during a trip to the pond."

"I don't know where you got your information," Michel said, his impatience with the man driving him to his feet. "But Prince Maximillian has remained on the palace grounds during his lessons. He was provided with a palace escort during his trip to the pond. His tutor has been protective of him. In fact, she injured her foot during the trip. More important, her methods have produced better results than I had hoped for. If the tutor should take Prince Maximillian beyond the palace grounds, I can assure you that security will accompany them." He nodded toward Faus. "That should settle your concerns."

Faus gave a slow nod. "Yes, Your Highness. But I'm not sure it's appropriate for Prince Maximillian to be running barefoot on the grounds. This tutor does not appear to be a proper influence in terms of propriety."

One of the things that irritated the hell out of Michel was the way everyone felt they should make decisions about how his son was raised. "The tutor is providing Maximillian with invaluable tools that he will need throughout his life."

"But propriety—"

"Propriety isn't always the top priority. Maximillian will have countless opportunities to focus on propriety. He's learning quickly, and he's happy."

"Happiness is not a priority in Prince Maximillian's training."

"I'm his father, and it's a priority for me. Maximillian is more productive when he's happy."

"With all due respect, I understand your concern for Prince Maximillian as your son, but Prince Maximillian also belongs to the people."

Michel felt his blood pressure climb. In the back of his mind he could imagine Maggie's response. *Butt out!* The thought calmed him, enabling him to speak his mind somewhat diplomatically. "It's my job as his father and his ruler to balance his future responsibilities with the development of his character. I appreciate your support of my judgment as I carry out both of these roles."

Faus gave a slow dip of his head and dismissed himself. As soon as he left, Nicholas rolled his eyes. "God, what a pain. Why don't you fire him?"

"It's not yet within my authority to get rid of him," Michel said, shoving his fist into his pocket. "While mother has passed on most of the responsibilities of the ruling position, I'm not officially *it.*"

"So you've got all the work but not all the perks," Nicholas concluded. "Bummer. When do you think Mother, dear, will toss the crown in your direction?"

"I think she's waiting for me to marry again."

Nicholas made a face. "What a choice. Marry someone the advisors choose or put up with their endless yammering. I don't envy you, brother. How do you stand it?"

Michel knew that none of his brothers envied him, yet for all the frustration of his position, most days he wouldn't trade it for the world. He gave a wry chuckle. "How do I stand it? I care. I care about Marceau."

"We're damn lucky then that you're in charge," he said. He studied Michel. "Just curious, what's up between you and Max's tutor?"

Michel tensed. "Nothing. She's American. She's entirely inappropriate." *Even though he thought about her entirely too often,* Michel mentally added.

"She's not hard on the eyes," Nicholas said.

"Just hard on a man's patience," Michel muttered, and raked a hand through his hair.

"But real. So you won't mind if I spend some time with her," Nicholas said.

Michel didn't breathe for a half moment. He rolled through every response he should make. He shouldn't care if his brother spent time with Maggie. He shouldn't care if she laughed with him. Or kissed him. Everything inside him rebelled at the thought. He could tell Nicholas to leave Maggie alone so she wouldn't be distracted from her job, but he wouldn't. He met his brother's gaze. "I would mind."

Nicholas looked at him for a long, considering moment, then gave a slow smile of approval. "Okay."

"Join me for dinner," Michel said to Maggie.

Sitting on her bed, she put down her book. "It's nine o'clock. I've already eaten."

"Then you can eat dessert," he suggested.

"Rough day?" she asked, not immune to his weary expression.

"Will you or won't you join me for dinner?"

"I will," she said, rising gingerly to her feet. She'd gotten wind of a portion of his day, and she'd have to be heartless to shun him at the moment. "How could a girl resist such a charming invitation?"

"I used all my restraint with one of my advisors today."

"I heard," she said, and limped beside him down the hall.

Michel threw a sharp glance at her. "From whom?"

"Dr. Nick. He checked my bandage today."

Michel relaxed slightly, then glanced at her foot. "Perhaps I should carry you."

She put her hands in front of her. "Oh, no. I won't win any ballerina contests, but I can get wherever we're going under my own steam."

"Take my arm, then," he said, extending his arm. When she hesitated, he raised a dark eyebrow. "Or I can carry you."

"Pushy, pushy, pushy," she whispered under her breath and allowed him to lead the way. They traveled down one hall, took two turns, then climbed a short set of stairs. "Where are we going?" she asked as he opened the door.

"My quarters," he said, and Maggie almost

turned around. He must have sensed her apprehension. "Chocolate-covered strawberries for dessert," he said, and led her into a plush but masculine room with carved mahogany furniture. On the west end of the room a serving table stood in front of a door to a balcony.

"That looks nice," she admitted. "I'm surprised you don't have a server."

"By the end of many days, I'm in no mood for polite conversation."

"Then why did you invite me?" she asked, using the term *invite* loosely.

"I knew you wouldn't be polite," he said, and grinned.

Maggie laughed in spite of herself. "Okay. Are we sitting on the balcony?"

"We are. I have some port to go with your chocolate, and after I eat dinner, I may smoke a cigar," he said as they moved onto the balcony terrace.

"That's nasty," she said, pushing the wooden cart onto the terrace. When she lifted the tray, he took it from her and set it on the table.

"Pardon?"

"I said that's nasty. Cigars are nasty, but I won't keep you from smoking one if that's what floats your boat. Heaven knows, you don't have a lot of room for vices." She took in her surroundings, the wrought-iron table and chairs with cushions, the bougainvillea and the view of the green garden below. "This is lovely."

"It's peaceful at the end of the day. Please sit," he said, gesturing to a chair, then he pulled his tie loose and took his seat.

He lifted the sterling cover from the plate and poured a glass of wine for both of them. On a china plate sat three chilled chocolate-dipped strawberries.

"Now, those are beautiful strawberries."

"Enjoy," he said, and his voice held a tinge of tantalizing seduction.

Unable to resist, she picked up one of the berries and inhaled the aroma of dark chocolate. She took a bite and closed her eyes at the delicious taste.

Sighing, she opened her eyes and caught Michel's gaze on her mouth. Her lips burned. She cleared her throat, tried to clear her mind and decided to broach a subject she had considered lately. "I think it would be a good idea for Max to learn to swim."

His fork stopped midmotion. "No," he said, simply, quietly.

"Why not? He's certainly old enough."

He swallowed another bite. "Safety issues."

"Safety?" she said. "You're teaching him to stab people with a sharp object and you're concerned about water safety?"

"That's different," he said.

"How?"

He sighed. "The swimming lessons have been delayed as a concession to my mother. One of my brothers drowned when he was three years old, and the family never really got over it."

Maggie felt a stab of empathy. "Oh, I'm sorry. That must have been terrible."

"It was. My mother overreacts at the mention of swimming lessons. The situation is complicated by the fact that my mother is the queen. The time is soon coming, however, when she will yield on this issue."

Maggie nodded, hearing the rock-hard resolution in his voice. "A difficult predicament, but since Marceau is surrounded by water, it makes more sense for Max to be protected by learning than ignorance."

"Agreed," Michel said, meeting her gaze, and she felt a connection resonate between them. When Michel looked at her, he really looked at her. She could almost swear he was searching her mind. The notion made her chest grow tight with an odd, unnamed emotion.

She took a sip of wine to break the intensity of the moment. "I understand one of your advisors was a pain today."

"Yes," he said, taking a bite of rice.

Her lips twitched. Even now he was reluctant to criticize the advisor. She found that both admirable and amusing. "How did you learn to be so diplomatic?"

"It took years," he said, taking a sip of wine and leaning back in his chair. "There are practical reasons for being diplomatic. One, you get less press if you keep a low profile and don't throw temper tantrums. Two, people tend to magnify and exaggerate things I say."

"But don't you find it incredibly stifling?"

"Sometimes more than others. I don't dwell on it. Presenting a boring outward appearance reduces hassle."

"But you're not boring," she insisted.

"How do you know?" he asked, his gaze falling over her like a warm breeze.

Her heart flipped, but she tried to ignore it. "Because you just aren't. You're intelligent, you're multidimensional, and..." she said, hesitating.

"And?" he prompted.

"And you have a huge ego, so I probably shouldn't say anymore," she said with a grin.

"No," he said, leaning forward, studying her. "What were you about to say?"

Maggie took a moment to collect her thoughts. Her thoughts and feelings for Michel were far more complicated than they should be, but she sensed, more than anything, Michel needed her honesty. Crazy to think such a man would need anything from her, but she suspected that he did. "I think what makes a person interesting is passion, and although you may not be emotionally demonstrative,

I get the impression you're very passionate about Marceau and your son, and your family." She lifted her glass to him in a slight toast. "But we digress from my original subject about your advisor. I understand he was mean. Would you like me to beat him up?"

Michel leaned back his head and laughed, and the sound shivered down her nerve endings. He looked at her and shook his head. "The queen would not approve of you."

She tilted her head to one side, uncertain how she felt about that. "I guess it's a good thing I won't be around long enough to try to impress her."

His smile faded, and he took another sip of wine. "You have no wish to marry me, do you?"

She looked at him in consternation. "Absolutely not," she said. "It's nothing personal," she added hastily. "I mean, you're handsome and very intelligent. Your sense of humor needs a little work, and you're a bit bossy, but most men in your position would be. You don't appear to have any terrible habits, and I imagine you're great in the sack, but—"

He made a choking sound. "Pardon?"

She rolled her eyes. "Ego, ego, ego. Men are all alike," she muttered. "I said, I imagine you're great in the sack."

"What makes you say that?"

"Well, the way you kiss," she said, feeling a rush

of warmth at the memory of the kiss they'd shared. "You kiss like nobody's business," she said, feeling her cheeks heat because she'd run off at the mouth. "But there's a flip side, and it's your job. Your schedule is worse than a doctor's. On call twenty-four hours a day, 365 days a year with a thousand suffocating rules."

"Thank you for reminding me," he said in a dry tone.

"Sorry," she said. "Was I supposed to make you forget?"

"Yes," he said with a nod and an expression in his eyes that did strange things to her stomach.

"How was I supposed to do that?" she asked.

He reached across the table, took her hand and gently tugged. The pull was an invitation, not an order, and the gentle insistence of the gesture slid past her defenses.

He held her gaze as she rose from her chair to stand in front of him. His title did nothing for her, but the man drew her, in a deeply elemental way. Her defensiveness dipped still more. She bit her lip. "I'm all wrong for you," she warned him. "Your advisors would advise you to stay away from me."

"I've disagreed with the advisors more than once. They've been wrong more than once." His gaze hardened slightly, hinting at the dangerous steel his smooth exterior belied.

He lifted her hand to his lips, then turned it over

and brushed his mouth against the inside of her wrist.

Her heart stuttered. She felt as if she were in quicksand and sinking fast. *Help!* she begged her rational mind. A mixture of desperation and arousal clouded her mind. ''I think I know what you need.''

His gaze burned her inside and out. ''What?''

''A chocolate-covered strawberry.''

Six

Without missing a beat, Michel said, "Then feed one to me."

Her mouth went dry. She hadn't been prepared for that response. Then again, her mind was so muddled she was doing well to plan her next breath.

"Feed one to me," he said, with just a hint of challenge.

Better the strawberry than her, she supposed. Tearing her gaze from his, she took a berry from the plate and gingerly lifted it to his lips.

He slid his tongue over the bottom and nipped the edge. The movement was so sensual she was sure her temperature rose three degrees. When he sucked a portion of the fruit into his mouth, she bit her lip. It was too easy to imagine his mouth doing the same kind of wicked things on her body. A piece of the chocolate cracked loose.

"You need to hurry or I'll drop it," she said.

"You're not close enough," he told her, and with a quick tug, Maggie found herself in his lap. He closed his hand around hers guiding the delicacy into his mouth in the same way she suspected he would guide her through lovemaking.

His gaze held hers as he took one last bite, then drew her finger into his mouth. The gesture was so blatantly sensual she closed her eyes.

"Look at me," he urged.

She opened her eyes to slits. "I'm trying very hard to stay rational here, and you're not helping."

"I find that when I keep hitting a wall, I need to try a different approach."

"I hesitate to heed your advice on this issue," she said, her voice wryly husky. "It's a little like taking Max's advice during a game of chess."

"Then I'll offer the same advice I think you would give me in this situation."

She was caught between extreme curiosity and arousal. "What would that be?"

"Forget rational," he said, and pulled her mouth closer.

"You are just too dangerous," she accused him

breathlessly. "You give this impression of being totally rational and careful. Prince perfect."

"So you know my secret. I'm a man with a man's needs. And I want you," he told her, and took her mouth. Splaying his fingers through her hair, he guided her lips over his. She felt totally surrounded by his warmth and strength, as if she sat in a sensual cocoon that consisted of the way Michel felt, tasted and smelled.

Still kissing her, he shifted her slightly so that she straddled his lap. He pressed his hand against her back until her belly was flush with his. Though they were both clothed, she was acutely conscious of the way her inner thighs hugged his hips.

He slid his hands down her arms, then to her hips. He pressed his palms against the bare skin beneath her shirt, and she shivered at the seductive sensation. He boldly skimmed his hands up the sides of her breasts.

Her heart hammered in her throat. "What are you doing?"

His eyes and hands did the talking, and they said he was totally focused on her. His intense, undivided attention did terrible things to her ability to think and breathe. He released her bra and caressed her breasts with his fingers.

"Come closer," he said, and the undertone of need in his voice took down her defenses. He was the most powerful, fascinating man she'd ever known, yet he wanted her. Everything about him represented her most forbidden, seductive dare. He was a dark winding road that she couldn't pass by.

She kissed him while he stroked her nipples to taut little peaks of pleasure. Her breasts grew swollen, and a decadent need built inside her.

Lifting her shirt off, he moved his mouth from her lips to her breasts and shifted his hips for better access. As he licked her nipples, he rocked intimately against her. Through her shorts and his slacks, she felt his hardness stroking her, heating her, and it was all too easy to imagine sitting on his lap with nothing between them. It was all too easy to imagine his strong thighs supporting her while he pumped inside her.

She couldn't swallow her moan. He slid his hands beneath her shorts and gently squeezed her bottom while he moved her over him. She unbuttoned his shirt and filled her palms with the touch of his rock-hard muscles beneath smooth, hot skin. The scent of sensual madness filled the night air.

"I want more," he muttered, his hands restless, as if he couldn't get enough of her. He took her mouth in a carnal kiss, his tongue seducing and blatantly mimicking a more basic joining.

Maggie had never felt such a driving need, a want that hinted at desperation. She heard a ringing in her ears and wondered if she was going crazy. The ringing continued, and Michel pulled his mouth from hers.

Her vision hazy, she stared at Michel while their harsh breaths rent the air. His eyes were black with sexual want, his lips swollen. The expression on his face was so honest it knocked on her heart and plucked at every feminine nerve ending in her body.

The phone rang again and he swore viciously. "I'm sorry," he said. "I must answer this. The only calls I receive in my quarters at this hour are of utmost urgency."

Her legs feeling like gelatin, she slid from his lap and nearly fell when she stood. Michel's hands shot out to steady her. "Okay?" he asked, his gaze searching hers.

Feeling entirely too vulnerable, she waved her hands. "I'll be fine. I just need to catch my breath. Please get the phone." *Please leave me alone, so I can get myself together.*

He left, and she drew in slow, deliberate breaths. She locked her knees as she moved to the edge of the balcony. Her hands shook as she grasped the rail. She closed her eyes, thankful Michel couldn't see her.

Refastening her bra, she felt her cheeks heat at how quickly he'd aroused her. He had found his way around her body in no time, and he could have easily taken her on the patio table within moments.

Maggie was definitely out of her league.

The only thing she'd ever done on a patio table was eat cheeseburgers.

"There's been a rock slide on one of our major roads traveling to the other side of the island," he said, the phone still in his hand as he stepped in the doorway. "I need to make a few calls to authorize immediate intervention."

A cold chill raced through her. "Was anyone hurt?"

"Injuries, but no fatalities yet."

"Is there anything I can do?" she asked, then immediately answered her own question. "I can get out of here, so you can make the calls."

She tripped over the leg of one of the chairs. Michel reached out for her, but she jumped back so he wouldn't touch her.

"Oh, no," she said in a voice that sounded high-pitched to her own ears. Heaven help her, she needed a clear head. She bit back an oath. She wished she didn't feel so jittery.

"I'm sorry we were interrupted," he said.

"It was probably for the best," she said, avoiding his gaze as she moved past him in the doorway. "We went a little further than I, uh, think was wise."

He shook his head, put his hand on her arm and pulled her against him. "*Au contraire, chère,* I would have preferred we go much further. And we will," he said as if he were making a promise.

* * *

Max made terrific progress on his lessons during the next few days, but Maggie could see he was longing for another adventure. Her foot still wouldn't allow anything involving water, so she enlisted Francois's reticent help.

"Done," Max said as he completed his last worksheet for the day. He drummed his pencil against the desk and glanced out the window. "We still can't go to the pond, can we?" he asked glumly.

Maggie rubbed his cowlick and smiled. "No, but we can go for a drive."

Max looked at her in disbelief. "Security is going to let *you* drive *me?*"

She made a funny face at him. "No, but I'll have you know I'm an excellent driver. Especially in countries where cars are driven on the right side of the road," she insisted as she stood. "No, some guy named Hans is driving, and another guy is riding shotgun. Francois is coming along, too."

"This sounds like a lot of fun," Max said in a doubtful tone.

"Would you rather stay inside the palace?"

He met her gaze. "No."

"Then you can be my tour guide. I'll bring along a few books in case you get bored. Francois says you have to dress just in case someone sees you. I'll do the same and meet you in ten minutes." As she walked toward her room, Maggie wondered why

GET FREE BOOKS and a FREE GIFT
WHEN YOU PLAY THE...

SLOT MACHINE GAME!

Just scratch off the silver box with a coin. Then check below to see the gifts you get!

YES! I have scratched off the silver box. Please send me the 2 free Silhouette Desire® books and gift for which I qualify. I understand I am under no obligation to purchase any books, as explained on the back of this card.

326 SDL DFTV

225 SDL DFTU
(S-D-OS-11/01)

NAME   (PLEASE PRINT CLEARLY)

ADDRESS

APT.#   CITY

STATE/PROV.   ZIP/POSTAL CODE

7	7	7	**Worth TWO FREE BOOKS plus a BONUS Mystery Gift!**
🍒	🍒	🍒	**Worth TWO FREE BOOKS!**
♣	♣	♣	**Worth ONE FREE BOOK!**
🔔	🔔	🔔	**TRY AGAIN!**

Visit us online at www.eHarlequin.com

DETACH AND MAIL CARD TODAY!

The Silhouette Reader Service™ — Here's how it works:

Accepting your 2 free books and gift places you under no obligation to buy anything. You may keep the books and gift and return the shipping statement marked "cancel." If you do not cancel, about a month later we'll send you 6 additional novels and bill you just $3.34 each in the U.S., or $3.74 each in Canada, plus 25¢ shipping and handling per book and applicable taxes if any.* That's the complete price and — compared to cover prices of $3.99 each in the U.S. and $4.50 each in Canada — it's quite a bargain! You may cancel at any time, but if you choose to continue, every month we'll send you 6 more books, which you may either purchase at the discount price or return to us and cancel your subscription.

*Terms and prices subject to change without notice. Sales tax applicable in N.Y. Canadian residents will be charged applicable provincial taxes and GST.

If offer card is missing write to: Silhouette Reader Service, 3010 Walden Ave., P.O. Box 1867, Buffalo NY 14240-1867

BUSINESS REPLY MAIL
FIRST-CLASS MAIL   PERMIT NO. 717-003   BUFFALO, NY

POSTAGE WILL BE PAID BY ADDRESSEE

SILHOUETTE READER SERVICE
3010 WALDEN AVE
PO BOX 1867
BUFFALO NY 14240-9952

NO POSTAGE
NECESSARY
IF MAILED
IN THE
UNITED STATES

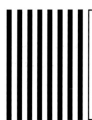

Francois felt she and Max needed three palace escorts for a little drive. Geez, did he think she would really cause an international incident?

A gleaming black Mercedes took them through colorful streets and past azure-blue waters. Max pointed out government buildings and the hospital that bore his late grandfather's name. As they drove past a road blocked off for construction work, Maggie studied the scene.

"Is this where the rock fall took place?" she asked, ducking to look up the winding road now mostly cleared.

Francois nodded. "Yes, it's a priority of Prince Michel to improve the island's infrastructure. The economy is changing."

"My father wants to try to find a way to bring in new businesses to make more jobs for people."

"Oh, looks like a clinic," Maggie said, taking in the small but lovely white building.

"Some of the children who were victims of the rock fall are recovering there," Francois said.

An idea sprouted in Maggie's head. "I'd like to stop," she said.

Hans slowed the vehicle.

"We cannot stop," Francois said. "A stop is not on our itinerary."

"Just for five minutes," she said. "I could give a few of these books to the children."

"I want to go, too," Max said.

Francois sputtered. "Absolutely not. It may not be safe."

Maggie shot him a look of disbelief. "A clinic? It's not as if it's a brothel."

"What's a brothel?" Max asked.

Francois glared at Maggie. "I knew this was going to be trouble. You promised."

Impatience stung her. "Oh, for Pete's sake, what can happen? The bodyguards can check out the place first, escort us in, and Max can learn a little lesson about charity. Do you really want to discourage His Highness from doing something good for the citizens of his country?"

Francois gave a heavy, unhappy sigh and continued to glare at her. He said something in another language to Hans, who then proceeded to pull the car into the tiny parking lot beside the clinic. Hans and Francois went into the clinic while Rolf sat in the car with Maggie and Max.

"Which books do you want to give away?" Maggie asked Max.

Max's face fell. "These are my favorites."

Maggie's heart swelled so tight she thought it could burst. Less than two weeks ago, Max had hated books. Now he had favorites. "Well, let's suppose I could replace all of them within a week, which would you like to donate?"

"You're sure you can get more?"

"Certain."

He shrugged. "Then I guess I can give away all of them."

She covered her heart. "You are growing to be such a fine man."

He was silent for a moment. "Think so?"

"Oh, I know so."

He sat up straighter and watched the window, squirming with excitement. Francois returned and opened the car door. "We will only stay for five minutes. We will visit no more than four patients. We will leave when I say. No arguments," he said, shooting a meaningful glance at Maggie.

Maggie nodded. She would have preferred a fifteen-minute visit, but since Francois was acting as if she'd asked for the crown jewels, she would be happy with five minutes. She bent down to Max and whispered in his ear, "Tuck in your shirt and be your nice self. They'll love you."

As soon as they entered, Maggie watched a line of nurses bow and murmur, "Your Highness." The excitement and curiosity on their faces was apparent.

"Thank you," Max said with a nod. "Good afternoon. I would like to meet some of the children who were hurt by the rock fall."

A nun stepped forward and bowed. "Please come this way," she said, and led the small entourage into a small room of girls with various injuries. Max shook hands with each of them and offered a book to the girls who could read. He made one last visit in another room where a little boy with a bandage wrapped around his head and another over his eye, lay in bed. "This is Ricardo. His family was in a truck when the rock fall took place."

"Your Highness," Ricardo said with excitement in his voice.

"It's a pleasure to meet you," Max said in his most proper voice. "Does your head hurt a lot?"

"It did, but it's better now, and they give us ice cream," the boy said with a smile.

"I get ice cream when I'm sick, too," Max said and extended a book to the boy. "Would you like a book? My teacher brought it from America. It's one of my favorites."

The little boy gaped in surprise.

"I hope you like it," Max said, then shot a grin at Maggie.

A camera flashed, and the bodyguard stepped in front of Max. "We must leave now," Francois said with a frown.

"Thank you, Your Highness," Ricardo said.

"À bientôt," Max called as Francois hustled him out of the clinic.

"I knew something would go wrong," Francois fretted as he helped Max into the car.

Maggie shook her head. "What went wrong? Max was great."

"The photo," Francois said. "The prince will be furious."

"Which prince?" Maggie asked.

"Prince Michel," he said impatiently. "He doesn't like Max's photo taken without permission. It's a protective policy," he explained to Maggie.

"Oh," she said, understanding why Michel would want to guard Max's privacy, although in her opinion, Max had a little too much privacy and isolation. "Maybe it won't turn out," she said. "Or maybe the person who took it will save it for their grandchildren and not want to share."

The photo was on the front page of the evening paper. Maggie and Francois were summoned to Prince Michel's office.

Michel didn't look pleased as he stood and held the newspaper. His brother Nicholas sat on a love seat and shot Maggie a look of sympathy.

Michel held out the front page. "I want an explanation."

Maggie tilted her head and looked at the enlarged photo. The two boys were smiling from ear to ear. Her heart melted. Heaven help her, she was growing to love Max. "Those smiles are incredible, aren't they?"

Michel glanced at the photo and met her gaze. "That's not the point. I have a policy concerning photos taken of my son. Why was this policy ignored?"

"I'm sorry, Your Highness. I accept responsibility," Francois said in a martyred tone.

Maggie frowned. "It's not Francois's fault. I twisted his arm into letting us go for a drive because I could tell Max felt cooped up. When we saw the clinic, I thought it would be a great lesson for Max to visit the injured children, and I badgered Francois into doing that, too. We were in the clinic for a whopping five minutes with two bodyguards that looked like they belonged in the World Wrestling Federation. No one expected the photo. My fault. If you're going to tear a strip off someone, Your Highness, it should be me."

Michel paused, then turned back to Francois. "Mademoiselle Gillian was not familiar with my policy regarding photos of Prince Maximillian. You were."

"Yes, I was, Your Highness, and—"

Although Francois drove her nuts at times, Maggie couldn't bear for him to take the heat when it was rightfully hers. She stepped in front of Francois. "It's not his fault. Even if I'd known your policy about photos, I probably would have made the same decision. Max did something good and felt good about it. Besides, it's a terrific photo."

"What if it had been terrible and Maximillian had been forced to relive the viewing of it a hundred times through countless reprints throughout his life?"

Maggie's heart sank. "That wouldn't be much fun. I don't suppose you can issue an order about bad pictures, can you?"

"No," he said curtly. "I can't."

"So you try to limit his exposure with boring official palace photographs, right?"

She heard Francois give a sharp intake of breath at the same time Michel nodded.

"But the public will eat this up with a spoon," she said. She thought about all Michel had said, and felt a heavy sinking realization inside her. "I've been as bad as your advisors, trying to tell you how to raise your son. You have your reasons. I may not totally agree, but I would never want Max hurt. Never," she said, feeling tears sting her eyes. "I'm so sorry."

She saw a flash of warmth in his gaze, but he only nodded at her. He glanced over her shoulder at Francois. "Francois, Mademoiselle Gillian continues to present new opportunities for Max. I commend you for your creativity in balancing her ideas with palace security."

"Just one more thing," Maggie said, and heard Francois make a choking sound behind her. "I can see why the photo issue is a big deal, and I think it's wonderful that you want to protect Max, but I'd hate to think he can only go out at night because he's forbidden to have his photo taken. There's an-

other way to protect him, and that would be culti-
vating a sense of humor.''

"Are you finished?" Michel said more than
asked.

"I guess so," she said, feeling as if someone had
let the air out of her balloon.

"I will take your suggestion under advisement,"
Michel said formally.

Her lips twitched as she remembered he used
those same words when he didn't like the advice he
received from the advisors. She was loath to be in-
cluded in that category. She sighed. "I'd rather you
were more direct and just tell me to stick it.''

Nicholas snickered, and Michel gave her a long-
suffering glance. "I will truly take your suggestion
under advisement.''

"Oh," she said, feeling a rush of surprised pleasure. "You're not just blowing me off. You mean
it.''

"Yes, I mean it," he said, his eyes glinting with
masculine humor while his lips remained straight.
She would have to ask him how he could make his
eyes smile when his lips didn't. Later.

Seven

This time when Maggie sneaked out of the palace after ten o'clock, she propped the door open with a flip-flop. She wore the other rubber sandal on her healing foot. Nicholas had told her the stitches should dissolve within the next few days. She inhaled the breeze and stared at the full moon.

Michel had sent a message inviting her to his quarters for dessert and drinks, but she had demurred, saying she was tired. Actually, she was trying to be sensible. She was starting to care far too much for this royal dad and his son. Maggie could feel herself growing attached, and she knew she would be leaving in weeks. It was already going to be difficult to say goodbye to Michel and Max.

Her chest felt tight with those "missing" feelings she knew she was going to have. She breathed deeply and tried to allow the serenity of the evening to settle her.

"I thought you said you were tired," a male voice from behind her said, making her jump.

She reeled around. "You walk very quietly for a prince," she accused, taking in the sight of his chest beneath his unbuttoned shirt.

"How is a prince supposed to walk?"

"With a loud, arrogant stomp so everyone knows he's coming. So if they're complaining about him, they can stop before he sends them to the dungeon."

"You weren't complaining. You were looking at the moon."

She turned back around and tried to recover some of the serenity, but her heart was skipping like a stone on the water.

He moved just behind her so she could feel the heat of him. "I see you remembered to prop open the door this time."

"I'm a fairly fast learner about practical things," she said.

"Why didn't you come when I asked?"

Maggie felt her heart hammer in her chest. "I felt bad about not respecting your wishes about your son."

"Are we going to discuss the photo again?" he asked in a weary voice.

"We don't have to," she said. "But I don't compartmentalize real well."

"That's not the only reason you didn't come," he said.

She wouldn't expect such a man to be able to look outside himself and practically read her mind, but he could. "You're right," she said, still staring at the moon. "I have a problem."

He put his hands on her shoulder and turned her to face him. "I can fix it," he said with entirely too much confidence.

"No. I think you might make it worse."

He dipped his head in disbelief.

"Don't tell anyone, but I think I might be starting to like you and Max too much," she finally whispered.

His gaze softened and he lifted his hand to her cheek. "Oh, Maggie, that's no problem."

"Maybe not for you," she said. "But it is for me. I'm going away in a few weeks and I'm going to miss the devil out of you two."

"You think we won't miss you?" he asked.

"Not like I'll miss you," she confessed, voicing a forbidden fear.

"You're wrong. Besides you could stay."

"My assignment will be over—"

"It doesn't have to be over," he said, his gaze dark with secret emotion. "Your assignment can be extended. I can take care of you."

Mistress. "But that's so sleazy," she said.

"Pardon?" he said in disbelief.

"The mistress, kept-woman thing. I'd rather be your friend. I'd rather be someone you can be yourself with. The biggest, best gift you can give me is to be real with me. To laugh when you're amused, to yell when you're angry."

"I don't yell very often. A lack of restraint shows a lack of power."

"Power shmower," she said. "This isn't about being princely. It's about what you really, truly feel."

He stood silently for a long moment. "I really truly want to make love to you all night long," he said in a low, urgent voice that tied her in knots at the same time it undid her.

Her breath left her lungs. "I'm going to have to think about this," she said. "When my brain works again."

"When will that be?" he asked with an edge to his voice.

"When you're not within twenty feet of me."

He looked deeply into her eyes and shook his head. "I'll find a way for you to stay," he said. "I'll find a way to make you want to stay."

"The last one isn't the tough one," she said, and gave into the silent demand in his gaze and kissed him.

* * *

Two mornings later Michel heard a tap at his door, then his assistant announced Maggie. Michel nodded, and she rushed into the room like sunshine. His heart lifted at the sight of her, although he suspected she might not like his news.

"Good morning, Your Highness," she said with a bright smile. "You rang? No wait, I want to show you something first." She extended a sheet of paper for him to view. "Max's signature. Isn't it great? I'm so pleased with his improvement."

Surprised and pleased, Michel studied the paper. "Max hates to write."

"Hated," she said. "Past tense. I made a little game of it. I told him that since he was going to be very famous, everyone was going to want his autograph, so he needed to start practicing so he would have a dynamite signature."

"Clever. No surprise," he said.

"Thanks," she said, her gaze holding his. "Your Highness, may I invade your space?"

A mix of curiosity and excitement clicked through him. The woman had invaded his mind. Hell, she might as well invade his space. "Yes," he said.

Maggie stepped forward and put her arms around him, then looked up at him and pressed her warm soft lips to his. He felt as if something inside him sighed with relief and pleasure. She felt so right in his arms.

She pulled back. "You looked like you needed that."

He couldn't deny it, but it didn't make what he was about to tell her any easier. "I called you to my office for a reason. I have a visitor coming this afternoon and I didn't want to take you by surprise."

She shrugged. "You have visitors all the time, don't you?"

"Frequently," he said with a nod. "But not quite like this one. We're having a party tonight in honor of her visit."

"Oh, I know. Max has asked me to come with him, so I borrowed a dress from one of the administrative assistants' daughters."

Michel ruthlessly pushed aside the seed of regret growing in his belly. "This is the daughter of an Italian count. Her father is highly influential in the government, and he is also an astute businessman. The advisors are quite impressed with her. She was educated in Swiss boarding schools and can speak three languages fluently. She's poised and even-tempered." He paused. "She is being considered as a wife for me."

Her eyes widened, and her jaw dropped. "Oh," was all she said aloud, but he could practically see the wheels in her brain spinning so fast they smoked. She turned away, and that small gesture sliced at him. He watched her take a breath as if to compose herself, then turn back to him.

"I just really hope you'll make sure she likes Max. He's such a terrific kid he deserves people who see that," she said.

"This is not a fait accompli. Isabella is a prospect," Michel told her. "But she will be a guest this weekend, and I thought it fair to inform you."

She nodded vigorously "Very fair," she said. "So I won't be expecting to spend time with you."

"You don't have to attend the party tonight," he said.

"Yes, I do. I told Max I would join him. But I'll be okay. It's not as if you can really pay a lot of attention to me in public, anyway. I mean, our relationship hasn't been and won't be public."

Michel wondered why his gut was clenching. "You need to understand that this is a political duty. There is no emotion involved."

She pressed her lips together, and her eyes turned sad. "Well, that's a darn shame. You do what you need to do, and I'll be okay," she said, and even though she stood mere feet from him, she could have been a million miles away. "Thank you for telling me."

He wanted to tell her that the visit had nothing to do with his feelings for Maggie, but he wasn't accustomed to having to explain himself in this kind of situation. "You're very welcome."

She nodded and walked to the door, then looked

over her shoulder as she was leaving. "I hope she makes you laugh."

That night Maggie put on her full armor. Full-length strapless turquoise dress with a slit, sexy sandals, mascara, eye shadow, blush, lipstick and perfume.

She felt like an amateur compared to the Italian visitor, Isabella. The woman wore a wispy chiffon, had a body that made Maggie rue the chocolate croissant she'd eaten for breakfast, and she moved like a cloud.

Maggie plodded. As she danced with Max on the balcony, Maggie told herself it didn't matter. She would never be a prospect for the position of wife to Prince Michel Dumont, and she didn't want to be. If there was one job she was ill suited for, it was the job of a prince's wife.

"One-two-three, one-two-three," Max said, moving in a surprisingly smooth waltz as he held on to Maggie's hands.

"You're doing great. Are you sure you haven't done this before?"

Max shook his head vehemently. "Nobody made me but you."

Maggie felt a tap on her shoulder.

"May I?" a male voice asked.

She turned to face Nicholas and felt a whisper of

relief. Maggie smiled despite her inner turmoil. "Did you want Max or me?"

Nicholas laughed. "You. I want to see how your foot acts under pressure."

"It's almost completely healed. Max, do you mind if I dance with your uncle?"

Max shook his head and pulled at his collar. "I'm gonna get a brownie," he said, and raced away from the balcony.

Maggie lifted her arms.

Nicholas took her arm and gestured toward the ballroom. "In the ballroom."

Maggie's heart sank. "Do we have to?"

He nodded firmly. "Yes." He led her nearly to the center of the floor, and they began to waltz.

"Is there a reason we couldn't stay toward the back of the room?"

"Yes, there is," Nicholas said. "I want him to see you."

"Who is him?" she asked innocently.

"My brother."

"Which one?" she persisted.

He shot her a look of disbelief. "Michel."

"You're not trying to cause trouble, are you?"

He shook his head. "No, but I think you're good for him. I don't want him to forget it."

Maggie looked past Nicholas's shoulder to the beautiful Isabella. "It would certainly be understandable if he did forget me. She's amazing, almost perfect.''

"Dull," he said. "She's had everything interesting drilled out of her. Michel would die of boredom. You're an excellent dancer. Everything about you sparkles tonight," he said. "Except your eyes."

Maggie tilted her head. "Are all of the Dumonts perceptive?"

"For the most part. In a position of authority it can be necessary for survival. Speaking of authority, did you know that although the queen has handed over most of the responsibilities to Michel, she has not given him the crown?"

Maggie shrugged and tried not to look at Michel. "No. Why should I?"

"No reason. She's waiting for him to marry again."

Maggie digested that fact. "Is there that much difference between being the official ruler and the unofficial ruler?"

Nicholas nodded. "When Michel takes the throne, he gets to choose his own advisors and set his own policies. Until then, he walks a tightrope between the queen's wishes and his own vision."

"Sounds challenging," she murmured, and her gaze caught Michel's. Her heart leaped and she looked away. Although she'd been carrying around a silly secret ache all evening, she hated that he felt pressured to marry. He led such a complicated life. "Why are you telling me all this?"

"Just making conversation."

The dance ended and the crowd applauded. An attractive man in military uniform approached Nicholas. "Your Highness, it's great to have you back."

Nicholas grinned. "John, it's good to see you. How is my brother treating you?"

"Working us like dogs," John said, glancing curiously at Maggie.

Nicholas raised his eyebrows. "Pardon my manners. Colonel John Bonaire, this is Mademoiselle Maggie Gillian from the United States. She's tutoring Maximillian. Maggie, John and I were friends in our teens. We both attended boarding school."

"*Enchanté,* mademoiselle," John said, taking her hand and brushing his lips over it.

"Thank you," she said. "It's nice to meet you," she said, then turned back to Nicholas. "What did you mean about how your brother was treating the colonel?"

"Ah, my second-oldest brother, Auguste. You haven't met him yet, but I'm sure you will. He's second in command of Marceau's military. He has a twin named Jean-Marc who is a special diplomat to Japan. Of course, my youngest brother, Alexander, is married and operates a yachting business. He spends most of his time in the States. And then there's Michelina, she's the baby."

Maggie's head swam with all the names. "I don't know if I can keep all this straight."

"When you get lost, just use 'Your Highness' and that will keep you out of trouble," John said with a smile. The music started again. "Would you care to dance?"

Maggie opened her mouth to say no thank you, but Nicholas interrupted. "Of course. She's a lovely dancer. Both of you enjoy."

Maggie shot him a dark look, but took a breath and danced with the colonel. A dance with the colonel turned into three, then two other men approached her. She finally begged off and headed straight for one of the men carrying trays of champagne. She was tempted to grab two glasses, but thought better of it and instead went in search of Max. She found him beside the dessert table.

"I'm afraid to ask how many treats you've eaten," Maggie said as she brushed the crumbs off his flushed cheeks.

"Just a few," he said, but gave a slight wince. "My tummy doesn't feel good."

"Oops, that sounds like more than a few," she said, gently urging him to his feet.

Hearing a slight commotion behind her, she turned.

"Oh, look, Prince Michel is introducing Isabella Garbanza. Aren't they the perfect couple?" the bystander said.

Her stomach twisted, but she pushed the sensation aside at the sound of Michel's voice.

"Ladies and gentleman, it is my great pleasure to introduce to you our honored guest from Italy, Isabella Garbanza."

The crowd applauded and Isabella smiled regally and nodded. "Definite princess material," Maggie muttered under her breath.

"What did you say?" Max asked.

Looking at his sweet face, she was struck by an idea. "Nothing, but there's one thing I want you to do before we leave."

His face brightened. "We're leaving?"

"Definitely," she said. "Have you met Mademoiselle Garbanza yet?"

He shook his head.

"I think you should go meet her."

Max looked at the long receiving line and made a face. "That's a long line."

She knelt down in front of him and looked into his eyes. "Usually you should take your turn like everyone else. That's the fair thing to do. But since your tummy hurts, we can make an exception."

"I can butt in?"

"Just this once. Be brief and whatever you do, don't heave on her dress."

Prince Michel was grinding his teeth so much his dentist was going to give him hell. Speaking of hell, where was the red-haired siren tutor who had danced with nearly every man at the party *except* him? He surveyed the crowd as he nodded absently at the people in the receiving line as they filed past him and Isabella.

Michel was just as irritated with himself as he was with Maggie. Isabella was beautiful, with impeccable manners and a soft-spoken voice. Her posture and carriage were perfect, she clearly understood European men, and she gave the impression she would be an undemanding mate. She was exactly what he'd wanted.

One month ago.

It was the party, he told himself. His entire point of view would change when he had time alone with her tomorrow. He nodded at another well-wisher in the receiving line, and suddenly he saw his son before him.

"Maximillian," he said in surprise.

Max bowed. "Hello, Father, good evening, Mademoiselle Garbanza. We are honored by your fine presence. Welcome to Marceau."

Michel's chest swelled with pride. "My son, Maximillian," he said to Isabella.

She dipped her head and gave a perfect smile. "Thank you for your kind welcome, Your Highness. It's a pleasure to meet you. Aren't you up a bit late?"

"Oh, I'm getting ready to leave. Mademoiselle

Maggie told me to greet you. She's leaving with me. Good night," he said, and ran through the crowd.

Michel stared after him and found Maggie. Her gaze met his across the crowded room. She smiled, imperfectly but sincerely. When Max caught up with her, she bent down and hugged him. He could well imagine her words of praise. An odd emptiness gnawed at him.

"Your Highness," said Isabella in her dulcet tones. "May I ask who is Mademoiselle Maggie?"

"Maximillian's tutor."

She smiled, again perfectly. "How broad-minded of you to include the help."

By the time Maggie read five books to Max, his tummy ache was gone and he fell right to sleep. When Maggie turned out her own light and lay down, every time she closed her eyes, the image of Michel and Isabella standing together and smiling appeared. They had looked so perfect together they could have modeled as figurines for the top of a wedding cake.

She tried to blot out the image and concentrate on the fragrant breeze, but her sheets felt scratchy. She felt restless and irritated. Another image of Michel and Isabella popped up. A knot formed in her chest. Would Michel tell Isabella his secrets? His true feelings? Maggie felt jealous and inferior and she was angry with herself for feeling that way.

Michel would never be hers. He never should be hers. Fighting the terrible, stupid feeling of loss, she tossed and turned for hours until she drifted into a restless sleep.

The following day Maggie was determined not to sit and mope. Max was scheduled to play with his cousins, so Maggie visited the market, then popped into an adult reading class at a library. The teacher welcomed her with embarrassing gratitude, but Maggie soon sat down to work with two of the adults learning to read. After the class, Maggie agreed to send along some educational materials before she departed Marceau.

She left the library feeling more in control of herself. The class had provided a welcome distraction. Still not inclined to return to the palace, she took a cab to the beach and walked along the shore. She sat on the sand and watched the sunset, then enjoyed an early dinner alone in an Italian restaurant. The host took pity on her and made conversation while she ate. He was an older man who spoke in broken English, but his kindness felt like a warm salve to the ache she'd been trying to escape.

By the time she returned to the palace it was nearly ten o'clock and she was tired. It took some doing to get past the guards, but she finally succeeded and trudged through the halls to her room. She opened the door to find the silhouette of Michel standing in front of her bed.

* * *

"What on earth are you doing here?" she asked.

"Where have you been?" he demanded, relieved as hell that she was okay, but angry that she'd worried him.

"To the market, library, beach and dinner," she told him. "You still haven't answered my question."

"With whom?" he asked, ignoring her questions.

Confusion crossed her face. "With whom what?"

"You went to dinner with whom?"

She lifted her chin. "With myself. Who did you have dinner with?"

"Myself," he said, anger oozing through him. "Isabella's visit was a failure."

Her eyes widened in surprise. "Why? She's beautiful."

"Yes," he said curtly, running a hand through his hair.

"She's perfect."

"Not exactly," he said, pacing the length of her small bedroom. "She's a snob."

Maggie winced. "Oh, sorry."

"But that wasn't her worst crime," he said.

"What was?"

"She wasn't you."

Eight

She wasn't you.

Maggie's heart felt as if it had stopped. She tried to breathe but couldn't. "What are you saying?"

He moved closer to her and touched her cheek. "That you have ruined me, *chère*," he said in a dark, sensual voice.

Maggie swallowed over a lump in her throat. "Should I apologize?"

"I couldn't even kiss her."

A wicked relief rushed through her. She bit her lip. "How terrible," she said, unable to keep the joy from her voice.

He shook his head and drew her forehead against

his. "Then you made it worse by disappearing today."

"I told Francois some of my plans."

Michel frowned. "He didn't mention them to me."

"I couldn't stay here. All I would have done was mope." She closed her eyes. "I hate being jealous."

"I couldn't tell you were jealous, especially when you sent Maximillian to greet Isabella."

"If you married her, I wanted her to love him, too," she said, stepping into his arms.

"I'm not marrying her," he said, and immediately unzipped her dress and pushed it to the floor. Swearing under his breath, he unfastened her bra.

Maggie shivered at the scalding speed. "Fast," she said through a tight throat.

"Overdue," he muttered, and took her mouth. His lips consumed hers in a kiss that made her blood roar through her veins. He suckled, nibbled and licked at her lips at the same time his hands slid over her breasts with taunting familiarity. As if he knew how sensitive her nipples were, he barely brushed them with his fingers, then moved away until she was aching for more.

The scent of unspent passion hung in the air, and Maggie was rocked by the power that vibrated between them. He slid his hard thigh between her legs, a sensual masculine invasion that made her pulse beat faster.

It was a calm night outside, but she felt thunder and lightning inside her. There was a possessiveness in Michel's eyes that burned her to her soul. Something inside her, something older than time, pushed her toward him. She unbuttoned his shirt and pushed it from his shoulders. While he ate at her mouth, she skimmed her hands over his bare skin and felt his chest gently abrade her nipples.

She allowed her hands to travel over his hard abdomen and lower, to his hips and thighs. He stood very still as she drew her hand closer to the part of him that throbbed with arousal. She brushed her hand over him, once, twice and drank in the sound of his groan.

She unfastened his slacks and slid her hand down the front of his briefs. He was hard, and touching him so intimately made her dizzy.

Michel picked her up and laid her down on the bed. Standing before her with the moonlight playing over him, he stripped. The strength of his muscles made her feel protected. And the sight of his arousal jutting out proudly made her buzz in all her secret places. But the honest need in his eyes melted her defenses.

Something about him compelled her to give him everything she could. Although a part of her was afraid, she could not have turned away from him if she'd tried. He tossed a couple of packets of protection on the beside table, then joined her on the bed.

He lowered his head to taste her nipples and she gasped. He pushed her panties out of the way and began to fondle her intimately.

Maggie grew wet and restless with need.

"I love the sounds you make," he told her. "I love the way you move." He slid his finger inside, and she gasped again. He gave her a French kiss that obliterated everything but him from her consciousness.

Then he made a path of sensual destruction down her throat, to each of her breasts. He skimmed his tongue over her belly and rubbed his cheek over her femininity and placed a kiss on the inside of her thigh.

Maggie couldn't swallow, couldn't breathe.

With agonizing slowness he found her most sensitive place and rubbed his tongue over her. Maggie felt herself grow so swollen she feared she would burst. Then she did, shattering over the edge. She thought she was done, but he took her with his mouth again.

When she began to shake, he pulled on protection and pushed her legs apart. "Look at me," he demanded in a husky, rough voice. Holding her gaze, he entered her inch by excruciating inch.

She bit her lip at his size.

His eyes closed to slits of pleasure, and his nostrils flared. "*Ma chère,* you are so small."

"Not very experienced," she murmured, holding her breath and waiting to adjust to him.

His gaze moved over her possessively. "I'm glad." He squeezed her bottom, and she relaxed.

He plunged deeper, and she gulped.

"You're mine," he told her in a voice that sounded as if it could travel through universes and across seas. "Now you're mine."

He began the age-old rhythm. His passion was so fierce she needed some reassurance, some measure of tenderness. She reached for his hand, and he lifted hers to his lips, and her heart was lost.

She clung to him as he shook with release, and something told her she would never be the same.

The sunlight streaming through the window awakened Maggie early the next morning. Lifting her hand to cover her eyes, she squinted around the room. Her senses awakened slowly. She was naked beneath her white cotton sheet, and when she shifted her legs, her thighs and breasts felt tender. She inhaled deeply, recalling the way Michel had made love to her. She wondered when he'd left her and fought a stab of abandonment. She looked beside her on the bed. If she didn't smell just a hint of his masculine spicy scent, she could almost believe she had dreamed that he had been in her bed.

Maggie sat up and wrapped her arms around her knees. The morning was peaceful, but her heart was in an uproar. Well, she'd gone and done it this time. Made love with a prince. How was she ever going to get him out of her system now?

Maggie bit her lip, and her gaze snagged on a wall calendar. The date she would be returning to the States was circled in red, and it wasn't far away.

Her stomach clenched. Maggie had often grown attached to her students, but this was different. Too restless to remain still, she stood and pulled a robe around her. There were so many things she wanted to teach Max, so many things she wanted to make sure he experienced.

And Michel. She closed her eyes at the clench inside her. Maggie wanted to know everything about him, but she knew that would take more than a few weeks. It would take a lifetime. She thought of his position and the proper bride he must someday wed. Her heart sank at the thought, and she castigated herself for her feelings. She had no right. She was temporary to him. He was temporary to her.

Why had their lovemaking felt timeless?

She looked at the calendar again. It would take a lifetime to know him. How could she fit a lifetime into two weeks? What would be left of her heart if she did?

"Thank you very much, but no thank you," Maggie said as she set the satin-lined jeweler's box firmly on the table in Michel's private den.

Michel looked at her in surprise, trying to understand the hurt and anger shimmering in her green eyes. He opened the box and looked at the diamond bracelet inside. "You didn't like it?"

She pressed her lips together in a frown. "Let's just say it's not me."

"Would you prefer a different stone than diamonds, or a necklace?"

She sighed. "I appreciate the thought, but I really don't want jewelry from you."

Michel couldn't fathom a woman who didn't want jewelry. "Why ever not?"

She crossed her arms under her chest. "Aside from the fact that I'm not a big jewelry person, I don't want you giving me jewelry. If you want to give me something, then give me—" She broke off and shrugged.

"Then give you what?" he asked, stepping closer, determined to eliminate the distance she was putting between them. He wanted her wrapped around him the way she'd been last night.

"I just don't want jewelry," she said in a low voice after a long pause.

A ray of recognition broke through his confusion. "You felt I was paying you for making love with me," he said, feeling his temperature rise. "You don't want me to give you gifts."

She looked at him warily. "Not...not...jewelry."

"I wasn't paying you for making love to me," he

told her as he ground his teeth. "If I want to give you a token of my feelings for you, then I damn well should be able to do it."

Her gaze softened, and she lifted her hand to his cheek. "When I go home to the States, I don't want to take tokens back with me, Michel. I want to take enough memories to keep me forever."

His chest squeezed tight, and he covered her hand with his. "It's not necessary for you to return so soon," he said, and when she opened her mouth to argue, he shook his head. "I'll help you to see things differently."

She stared at him, then her lips twitched. "Oh, really, and how do you plan to do that?"

The dare in her eyes was a delicious tease he couldn't resist. "Just because you may not have a weakness for diamond bracelets doesn't mean you don't have a weakness for other things," he said, and guided her forefinger to his lips. He encircled the tip with his tongue and watched her bite her lip.

She cleared her throat. "Such as?"

"Chocolate strawberries," he said, drawing her finger into his mouth. She closed her eyes, fighting the arousal, but not winning, he noticed with a rush of gratification.

"And me." He picked her up in his arms and walked toward his bedroom. He had dreamed of seeing her there, her wild, red hair spilling over his pillow, her body naked on top of his sheets. Michel had never felt so possessive about a woman before, not even his wife. That thought could have bothered him, but not now. Now Maggie was in his arms, lifting her lips to his, and soon she would be his again, in the most elemental way.

Hours later she curled against him, both of them replete with lovemaking. He felt her nuzzle his throat, and he smiled. An exquisite contentment seeped through him.

"Tell me the story of Marceau," she said.

"Which story?"

She groaned. "The story of why your family got the job as rulers."

"Hundreds of years ago the Dumonts didn't rule. The Dumonts were cousins of the ruling family of Rocher. To make a long story short, the Rochers were not good money managers, and they often squabbled among themselves. Somebody was always trying to steal someone else's wife. There was a duel between the heirs to the throne and both were killed. The Dumonts protested the chaos the Rochers had created and threatened a takeover. The Rochers didn't want to lose everything, so they made a deal. Dumonts would take Marceau, and the Rochers would take the Gantos Islands."

She raised up on her elbow and looked at him in confusion. "But I thought the Gantos Islands belonged to France."

"They do. The Rochers took the Gantos Islands,

but they still had money problems, so after a time, they ended up being forced out for a chest of gold French coins that has never been accounted for.''

She widened her eyes. ''Whew, missing gold coins, wife stealing, political plots.'' She shook her head. ''And I thought my family was dysfunctional.''

He chuckled, thinking he liked the sight of her naked in his bed, with her wild hair spilling over her shoulders. ''Yes, but the Dumonts prevailed. What about your family?''

She made a face. ''We don't have any gold or political plots. I had a perfect brother who was the apple of my father's eye. My parents have been separated for some time, but they haven't divorced. I think they can't give up torturing each other. Even though I had problems in school, as I grew older, they turned to me to mediate and *fix* things. Not a fun job.''

''I can see not,'' he said, glimpsing a trace of pain and frustration in her eyes. ''You're not close to them now,'' he concluded.

''No. I keep in touch and visit on holidays and birthdays.''

''So it wouldn't be difficult for you to be away from them if you decided to stay on Marceau,'' he said, planting the thought the same way a farmer in his country would plant a vegetable crop. He had observed that Maggie responded well to planting.

She looked at him sideways. "Yes, but I have other reasons for going back to the States," she said. "I like being an American."

"You can have dual citizenship. We're very liberal in that way."

Her lips turned upward in a slow, but brilliant smile. "If you keep this up, I'm going to start thinking you really want me to stay."

"You could have a wonderful life in Marceau," he said. "I can make it happen."

She shivered, distracting him with the slight jiggle of her breasts. He loved the way her aureole felt in his mouth. Michel felt his body respond. It didn't matter that he'd just made love to her. He wanted her again.

"You're tempting," she said in a low voice. "But what happens when you decide you're in the mood for something different from a red-haired American woman who is not into jewelry?"

"That would take a damn long time," he said.

"And in the meantime I would have fallen desperately in love with you. And you would have to find a discreet way to ditch me. Then I would return to America and try to put my career and myself back together." She skimmed her hand over his jaw. "I think it would be very foolish to count on a relationship you and I might have."

Irritation nicked through him. "It would be foolish for you to underestimate my power in this."

"Your Highness, you have my utmost admiration and respect, and I know you have all kinds of power, but I have to continue to count on me, not you. In the end it's going to be just me."

His chest grew tight at her words. He wanted her to count on him. He wanted to be her protector. He wanted, and as much as she was giving herself to him, he wanted more. He ran his thumb over her kiss-swollen lower lip. "You have a lot to learn about me, but we have time."

She darted her tongue out over his thumb, surprising him with her sexual mischief. "Tell me what else I have to learn about the mighty Michel."

"That I'm not fickle," he said, meeting her gaze dead-on. "And I like to win."

"Max must have gotten the same qualities from you. He's not fickle. He wanted a dog when I first met him, and he still wants one now. He likes to win, and whenever I play chess with him, he does."

"The desire to win will help him with some of his royal duties. In just a few weeks he'll be expected to address the people on National Citizenship Day."

Maggie did a double take. "Address the people, how?"

"It's tradition," he said, still distracted by her breasts. "All seven-year-old heirs to the throne make an address on National Citizenship Day. He will read a brief speech which will be recorded for radio and television.''

"Wait. Wait just a minute. Max is making terrific progress, but I wouldn't want to put him in front of a TV camera and tell him to read."

"You won't. You will just prepare him for it."

She pulled back and frowned. "Do you have any idea how difficult it can be for a dyslexic to read in front of a large group?"

"You do it all the time."

"Yes, but I know the tricks."

"You can teach them to Max."

"I think you should reschedule this for next year."

Michel laughed. "Even I can't reschedule Citizenship Day."

Clearly distressed, she made a sound of frustration. "But you don't have to make him do this."

"The people expect it. Max's appearance is not optional," he said gently, firmly. A part of him was deeply touched by her protectiveness of Max, but he also knew she would need to bend this time. "He will do fine with your help. It's part of the reason I hired you."

As if she knew she was batting against a stone wall, she sighed. "It's one of those royal-appearance duty things, isn't it?"

"More," he said. "Seeing Maximillian say his brief words gives the citizens of Marceau a sense of pride and assurance in the future. I don't agree with everything the advisors say, but Max will have many opportunities because of his position. He will also be required to perform duties because of his position."

"To whom much is given, much is required," she quoted and turned silent for a long moment. She eased back down to the crook of his arm as if she were mulling over her thoughts. "I think I wouldn't be a very good mother," she said.

He stared at her. "Why in heaven's name would you say that?"

"Because I think I would do just about anything to keep my child from hurting, and sometimes we all have to hurt a little in order to grow."

"You're very tenderhearted, *ma chère,* but you're also very strong. Your child would have your strength, too."

She gave a heavy sigh. "I should probably leave," she said, but didn't move.

Michel vehemently disagreed. "No," he said.

"Unlike you, I'm likely to fall asleep and not wake up. You'll have to kick me out of bed, and I'll end up getting my feelings hurt."

Realization echoed inside him. "You were hurt when I left last night," he said.

"Not really." She must've read the disbelief on his face. "Well, maybe just a little bit. A very little bit."

"I didn't want you to have to face the gossip from the palace employees," he told her.

Her gaze softened, and she swallowed hard, as if she were fighting a knot of emotion. "I hate to feed your ego, but you're right," she said with a lightness at odds with the intensity in her eyes. "There's a lot I don't know about you."

He pulled her face to his. "Stay and learn."

Nine

Two weeks! Two blinkin' weeks!

Maggie did her best to hide her dismay and frustration when she learned she had two weeks to help Max prepare for his public presentation. When she'd reminded him of the event, he'd gotten a sick look on his face. But Maggie was determined to make this a successful experience for Max, and in a way for Michel, even if it killed her.

Or even if Michel killed her when he learned the latest thing she'd done. He would probably need to get in line behind Francois and all the advisors, and the queen, too, if she were here.

She received the planned speech from the palace

PR people. It was three pages long with words inappropriate for a seven-year-old, so Maggie gently *edited* it.

Okay, she hacked it. It was now one and a half pages long. She rewrote it on a different computer and printed it off in a huge font on colored paper so it would be easy for him to read.

"This looks different from the first one they sent over," Max said, looking at the paper.

Maggie decided not to address the issue. "I think what we're going to do is have you memorize the speech."

Max's eyes widened in alarm. "The whole thing!"

Maggie nodded. "Don't worry. You have excellent memorization skills, and we're just going to do it in little chunks, two or three times a day."

Max gave a heavy sigh. "I'm going to be cooped up in this room for the next two weeks trying to memorize this."

"No, you won't," she assured him. "You and I are going to have a picnic by the pond today and we're taking the speech with us. You can think of it as eating one cookie twice a day, instead of eating the whole jar and getting sick."

"It's more like taking cough medicine," he grumbled.

She couldn't disagree. "Besides, I have ordered

a very special reward for you after you have finished memorizing the speech.''

Max perked up. "What kind of reward?"

"It's very special. It's a surprise." *To everyone* except me, she thought, and fought a little attack of nerves.

He studied her with curiosity. "Is it from America?"

She nodded. "Yes."

"Is it books?"

She shook her head. "No. It's something you've never had before. And I'm not going to tell you any more, so don't ask."

"Is it videos?" he asked slyly.

"Absolutely not," she said, shooting him a dark look. Max knew she didn't approve of vegetating in front of the television. "If you don't start memorizing, you'll never find out what it is because you'll never get it."

He gave a heavy sigh. "Is it—"

She held up the speech. "Don't ask."

Every night Michel insisted she join him in his private quarters. They made love, but they also talked of his dreams for Max and Marceau, and of his memories of childhood. He asked about her life in Washington, D.C., and was appalled when she casually referred to crime in the schools.

"If you insist on returning, I'll send a guard with you," he said, his light eyes blazing.

Maggie chuckled as she sat cross-legged across from him on the sofa. "I don't think Hans would go over very well with second-graders. Plus he probably wouldn't appreciate the assignment when the kids spill milk on him and smear him with peanut butter."

"Or you could decide to stay in Marceau and function as the national literacy representative."

Curious, Maggie met his gaze. "I've never heard of a national literacy representative," she said.

"It's a newly-created position. The literacy representative will work with the royal education advisor to facilitate literacy programs for both children and adults."

"Just out of curiosity, how new is this position?" she asked.

His eyes glimmered with humor and intelligence. "It was approved today."

Maggie looked at him, feeling a rush of emotion and frustration. What a power play to create a job to lure her to stay. On the other hand, how could she not fall for the man when he was creating a dream job for her in such a beautiful setting?

She crawled onto his lap. "You're making it very difficult for me to leave."

"That is my purpose," he said, his expression so sensual she found it hard to breathe.

"Why?"

"You would be very good for Marceau. I'm confident our literacy rate would increase exponentially."

"And that's the whole reason," she said. "Because I could do wonders for literacy. There's nothing personal at all."

His gaze darkened, and he lifted her hand to his lips. "I didn't say that. I want you close by." He slid his other hand behind her neck and took her mouth in a kiss that whispered secrets—secrets Maggie was afraid to believe. He tasted her and tempted her like a man determined to keep her. *He didn't just want her,* he needed her. The seductive possibility alternately thrilled and terrified her. How would her life be if she stayed? How much more of Michel would she grow to know and love? Wouldn't it be harder than ever for her to leave then?

The ghost of Maggie's future rang a warning bell. She kissed him with all the passion in her, but her heart was heavy. How could this possibly end well?

"On Citizenship Day, we celebrate the strength and determination of our ancestors who have kept Marceau at peace for over two centuries. We celebrate the commitment of our government to ensure that no one in Marceau should go hungry. We also celebrate the bright future to which each citizen contributes. I'm grateful and proud to be a part of this country where the people have such strength and heart. God bless Her Majesty, Queen Anna Catherine, His Highness, Prince Michel, and every citizen.''

Maggie's eyes filled with tears and she put her hand to her heart. She and Francois sat among the crowd of stuffed animals she'd created as pretend spectators for Max's performance. She began to applaud. "Bravo!" she yelled. "Bravo!"

Francois began to clap, too, and she heard him sniff. *"Magnifique!"*

Max beamed with pride and pleasure. "I did well, didn't I?"

Maggie went to hug his sturdy frame. "Oh…you *rock*," she said.

"What does *rock* mean?" Francois asked.

Max nodded. "It means you're the best."

Francois sniffed again. "Your father will be so proud. The queen," he said, his voice catching. *"Mon dieu,* the queen will be beside herself. The PR department outdid themselves with the speech."

"Oh, well, Mademoiselle Maggie helped—"

"But Max's delivery was what really made it all work," she said, not wanting to get into a snit fest with Francois over her revision of the speech. She had a veritable smorgasbord of snit fests to face in the coming twenty-four hours.

Max tugged at her arm. "When do I get my reward?"

"Very soon," she said. "I'm picking it up for you later."

"It has arrived from the States?" he asked, moving from foot to foot in excitement.

"What reward?" Francois asked warily.

"Oh, it's a surprise I promised Max when we first started working on the speech."

"What is this surprise?" he asked, his wariness turning to suspicion.

And rightfully so, Maggie thought, uneasiness twisting in her belly. "If I tell, it won't be a surprise," she said giving a meaningful sideways glance at Max. Heaven help her, she was the worst at subterfuge and evasion. "Very soon," she said, patting Max's cowlick.

Michel joined his advisors after dinner for an evening meeting in anticipation of the extended holiday before Citizenship Day. They had covered just about everything on the agenda when he heard a strange noise down the hall. The meeting continued, but so did the noise that he couldn't quite identify. He tossed a questioning glance at the male assistant standing by the door, and the assistant gave a nod and opened the door.

To a yipping sound that strongly resembled the sound a *dog* would make.

One of the advisors turned to him with a look of

surprise on his face. "Your Highness, is there a *dog* in the palace?"

Michel wondered who on earth would bring a dog to the palace, and his mind didn't have to travel far. *Maggie.*

"I'd like to call the meeting to a close and allow you gentlemen to begin your holiday. We've covered all the pressing matters. I do appreciate your attendance so late in the evening, and I look forward to your presence at the Citizenship Day celebration."

"Prince Maximillian will be speaking, won't he?" one of the advisors asked.

"Yes, of course, and I understand from his assistant that he's very well prepared." Prince Michel smiled. "We will all be proud." He stood, inviting no further questions. "Good night, all," he said, and left the room.

His assistant met him halfway down the hall where Michel heard raised voices. "Your Highness, there is a problem."

"I got that impression," he said, drawing closer to the recreation room. The dog's howling, along with the voices grew louder as he opened the door.

A beagle puppy, yipping and howling, sat cowering at Maggie's feet as she shook her finger at a red-faced Francois.

"Dogs are not allowed in the palace. They are forbidden by the queen," Francois shouted.

"It's too late to send him back," Maggie retorted. "I promised Max a reward for learning his speech, and the puppy is his reward."

"You should not have made that promise without consulting the palace authorities. You have really done it this time, Mademoiselle Gillian. The dog must go," Francois said, moving toward the puppy.

Her eyes glinting with sparks, Maggie raised her chin and her hands as if she were ready to take him on. "You just try it."

Time to step in before a full-fledged brawl breaks out, Michel thought. "Francois is correct," he said. "The queen does not allow dogs in the palace."

Maggie jerked around to meet Michel's gaze. He saw her resolution sink for just a second before she recovered. "Given the fact that she gave birth to several children, I'm not exactly sure how she escaped with no pets, but that's beside the point. The queen won't have to take care of him. The queen is not a seven-year-old boy who wants a pet so badly he sneaks tadpoles into his room. It's not as if he has a dozen friends or siblings to play with," she said, then, as if she suddenly remembered a smidgen of protocol, she bent her knees in a pseudo curtsy. "Your Highness."

"Puppies are noisy and messy. They disturb palace life."

"Babies are noisy and messy, too," she said,

matching him argument for argument. "Are they forbidden from palace life?"

Michel struggled with an overload of frustration. "Of course not," he said. "You should not have brought that dog into the palace without permission. Max is going to be disappointed when the puppy is removed."

"If I may say, it's wrong, wrong, wrong for that puppy to be removed. That puppy will inspire Max to read how to take care of it and develop a sense of responsibility. That puppy will provide companionship and friendship especially after I—" She stopped, clearly faltering at the thought of leaving.

Michel's gut twisted.

"Having the puppy will give him invaluable qualities throughout his life."

"You were not invited to say so," he said firmly.

Through the corner of his eyes, Michel saw Max peek through the doorway. He watched his son bend down and clap his hands at the beagle. The beagle apparently recognized his protector and skittered across the floor into Max's arms. Max picked him up and was rewarded on the face with puppy licks.

"Sir," Max said, looking at his father with beseeching eyes. "I'll do anything to keep the dog."

Damn, Michel thought. At this moment there was nothing in the world he wanted more than to give his son this simple wish. The problem was that he had bigger issues to broach with the queen, one of which was nonnegotiable for him. Michel had learned not to overwhelm the queen with more than one battle at a time.

"Put the puppy in the basement," he said crisply.

"In the dungeon?" Maggie asked, appalled.

"We don't have a dungeon anymore," he told her impatiently. "It's been remodeled."

"May I sleep with him?" Max asked.

"Absolutely not," Michel said. "If I find you disobey me on this, the dog will go."

"But he's just a puppy," Max said. "He'll be lonely."

"Then I suggest you study mademoiselle's puppy books to learn how to help him successfully make the adjustment." He glanced at Francois. "You will help Max with this."

Francois blanched. "Me?" he echoed, his voice breaking. He cleared his throat. "Begging your pardon, Your Highness, I know nothing about dogs."

"Due to Mademoiselle Gillian, it appears we will all be learning about dogs, whether we wish to or not."

One of the assistants cleared his throat. "If I may offer my assistance, Your Highness," he said. "My family had several dogs during my growing-up years."

"Most normal families do," Maggie muttered under her breath.

Michel shot her a quelling glance. "Thank you.

This is to remain strictly confidential until further notice,'' he said, then turned full bore on Maggie. ''Mademoiselle Gillian, meet me in my quarters.''

''When?'' she asked warily.

''Immediately,'' he said, and caught the faintest wince on her face as he strode out of the room toward his quarters. The anger roaring through his head drowned out any other sound.

As soon as he arrived at his door, he swung it open, waited for her to enter, then slammed it shut. Michel couldn't remember the last time he'd slammed a door. He was so angry he deliberately stood several feet from her. ''Do not ever undermine my authority again,'' he said.

Maggie flinched at the steel in his tone. ''I apologize, but I did it because I'll be leaving soon.''

''That is not decided,'' he said, feeling his frustration grow exponentially.

''Whether I go next week, next month or next year,'' she said, ''we both know I will eventually have to leave.''

''We do not know that,'' he said in a crisp voice.

She looked up at the ceiling as if she were seeking help. ''Listen…you can deny it until, well, in the States we say, until the cows come home. But when all is said and done and I return to my country for whatever reason at whatever time, nothing will change for you, but everything will change for me. So I can't be the queen of denial.''

She sighed and moved closer, tentatively reaching out to him. Michel didn't trust himself to let her touch him.

She dropped her hand to her side, and his heart felt as if it shrank.

"If I had it to do all over again, I would still get Max the dog. I'm sorry, but I just don't understand why a beagle needs to be a state secret or cause an international incident. I just don't get it, and this is why it will never work out for me to be here. When it comes down to a choice between protocol and what is going to make you and Max happy, I will always look after your hearts. Always," she said. "And that means I will always cause trouble."

Michel felt as if he walked a fraying tightrope. The rope would not hold much longer. His relationship with his mother had always been more professional than personal. Now was no different. At the same time the clock was running out for Maggie. Selfishly he refused to accept her departure. He might have sacrificed many other things for the sake of the crown, but he refused to let her go so easily. He needed time to collect his thoughts.

"The queen returns day after tomorrow. I will use the time to prepare for my meeting with her."

Maggie's gaze was warm with concern. "You have a lot on your mind."

It was strange as hell, but even though she'd just

complicated matters, her presence calmed him. "Yes," he said simply.

"Would you like me to leave?" she asked.

"No," he said immediately.

"Then what can I do? I knew there might be a few objections to the puppy, but I didn't want it to make things worse for you. Is there anything I can do to make things better?"

The longing in her voice to make it all better scored his heart and tempted him terribly. "Is it possible for you to follow instructions without arguing?"

Affronted, she shot him a dark look. "Yes, I can follow instructions without arguing."

He pulled his jacket off, then discarded his shirt. "Follow me," he said as he headed for his bedroom. "You can rub my shoulders," he said.

Maggie still had mixed feelings about his imperious tone, though the sight of his bare strong back had distracted her. She truly didn't want to cause trouble for Michel, and it appeared she had. If giving him a back rub would make him feel a little better, then she certainly wanted to do it.

He lay down on his bed and gave a heavy sigh as if the weight of the day had been great. Maggie suspected it had. Her heart squeezed at the thought. This was the man behind the crown, and he was tired and frustrated.

Amazing that she had the power to make him feel better. "Do you have any lotion?" she asked.

"I just want your hands," he said, and her heart gave a little jump.

She started with his neck, gently kneading his tensely corded muscles. Moving to his shoulders, she massaged, thinking that in many ways he carried a huge weight every day. She rubbed her way thoroughly down to his lower back. Slowly up again, she moved her hands to his shoulders and neck to his scalp.

He gave a murmur of approval when she moved her fingertips over his scalp. Maggie continued until she was certain he had fallen asleep.

Instead, he rolled over and met her gaze. "Take off your blouse," he said.

Confused, she searched his expression. "But I thought—"

"Are you arguing?"

Follow directions without arguing, she remembered, and took off her blouse.

"Now your bra."

She did, feeling slightly self-conscious. Her breasts reacted to the sensation of his gaze. "Touch my chest," he told her.

Leaning forward, she ran her hands over his muscular chest. The assignment was no hardship. His chest was beautifully masculine. She caressed him and slid her fingers through the soft hair in the center of his chest. With each touch she saw his breath deepened. The atmosphere changed. He might be giving the directions, but she felt a heady sense of feminine power.

He was becoming aroused.

So was she.

She skimmed her hand down to his belly and stole a glance at him. Lower and lower she trailed her fingers to just below the top of his slacks. Emboldened by the desire steeping in his eyes, she unfastened his belt and slowly unzipped. If she didn't know better she would swear Michel was holding his breath.

Part of her wanted to make love to him. Another part wanted to tease.

"Oops," she said, lifting her hand away. "I'm not following instructions."

"Yes, you are," he said, and his gaze melted her.

He looked at her breasts again, and his gaze felt like a seductive stroke. She lowered her mouth to his throat and kissed him. Her breasts meshed with his rib cage, and he gave a sigh of pleasure.

She pressed openmouthed kisses over his chest, sliding her tongue over his nipples, then French kissing his abdomen.

He removed his slacks and underwear, revealing his full arousal. He reached for her, but she dodged him.

"Maggie," he said, and the dark sexual need in his voice mirrored her own.

She shook her head and lowered her mouth to kiss the inside of his thigh. "I'm following your instructions."

"I haven't given you any," he said, plunging his hands through her hair.

"Your body has," she said, and rubbed her thumb from the base of his shaft to the tip.

"Maggie," he said again, this time his voice ragged around the edges.

Following a forbidden instinct, she replaced her thumb with her mouth and drew her lips up the length of him.

He swore and tangled his fingers more deeply in her hair.

Reveling in the sensation of his thighs against her bare breasts, she moved her head from side to side, rubbing her cheek over him, taking her time. Then she took him into her mouth, and he made the sexiest masculine sound she'd ever heard.

She felt herself grow moist between her thighs. She stroked him with her lips and tongue. The tip of his manhood turned shiny with the honey of his arousal.

Meshing her gaze with his, she lowered her head once more and swirled her tongue over him.

He swore as if the sight was too much for him.

It must have been. Before she knew it, he flipped

her over on her back and took her mouth. "I can taste me on you," he said as if it were an unbearable arousing experience, and he kissed her again. He played with the aching tips of her breasts and skimmed his hand down between her legs to find her wet and wanting.

"You feel so good," he told her. "So good," he said and lowered his mouth to her nipples. The sensation was excruciatingly wonderful.

Unable to hide her arousal, she arched against his mouth. He continued to touch her femininity as if he were stroking the petals of a rose. "I always want to take you too fast," he muttered, and took a deep breath.

Turning her on her side, he stroked her so that she felt his hardness rubbing against her bottom. With one hand, he stroked her nipple and the other, then he slid his finger inside her. She felt the strength of his chest at her back and the combination was oddly erotic. She undulated against him, and he groaned.

"I can't go slow if you're not still," he told her.

Maggie felt the heat inside her grow. Her body felt like a flower ready to bloom. She wanted him in every way.

"I don't want you to go slow," she said, and undulated again.

He groaned, and with one smooth, slick movement, he entered her femininity from behind.

She caught her breath at the exquisite pleasure. She wiggled and he slowly pumped, still touching her most sensitive spot. The combination was too much. She clenched around him and soared.

He thrust once more, deep inside her, and she felt his body shudder with pleasure. After several moments of trying to catch her breath, Maggie rolled over to face him.

His gaze was so intently possessive it took her breath again. "I like the way you give a back rub," he said, his voice rife with every intimate implication. "I like the way your hands and mouth feel. I like the way your breasts feel." He slid his hand over her waist. "I like the way you feel when you take me inside," he said, and kissed her.

Maggie felt as if she were utterly under his spell. Whatever he asked of her she wanted to do. She had never felt like that about a man, and feared it could be a dangerous situation. Her brain was too full of him at the moment to contemplate a way out, though. She was compelled to find a way to show Michel the depth of her emotion for him.

"I keep trying to find the perfect way to show you how I feel," she confided as she lifted her hand to his cheek.

"You're on the right track," he said, his eyes full of seduction. "Keep trying."

Ten

Before she'd left Michel last night, he'd instructed her to stay out of trouble for the next two days. He'd said it as if he'd thought that might be setting a new record.

In her attempt to be boring, Maggie joined Max as he brought the puppy up from the basement to take him for a walk outdoors. As they turned down a hallway, she and Max stopped at the sound of two women having a heated conversation.

"You're not old enough to go out with a man unchaperoned," a woman said.

"As far as you're concerned, I'll be eighty before you think I'm old enough," a younger woman retorted.

"It may well take you that long to mature," the other woman said. "I thought you would be pleased to join me on this diplomatic tour to America."

"I was," said the younger woman. "Thank you very much. Now I would like to return without an entourage."

Max's eyes rounded. "It's Queen Anna Catherine," he whispered. "And Princess Michelina. They're always arguing."

Panic sliced through her. "But she wasn't supposed to return until tomorrow," Maggie said.

Max shrugged his shoulders helplessly.

The voices drew nearer and Maggie glanced around, desperately seeking an escape. Spotting a closet, she hustled Max and the puppy inside and pulled the door shut behind them. "Please be quiet," she said to the puppy. "Please be quiet."

But it was dark, and the dog began to whine. "I'll hold his mouth together," Max whispered as the queen and her daughter drew nearer.

The dog let out a yelp, then another, and Maggie cringed.

"Is that a dog I hear?" the queen asked in disbelief.

The puppy barked again. Maggie glared at him. "You must have a death wish," she whispered, but the puppy just wagged his tail and barked again.

The door flew open, and Maggie found herself staring into two pairs of the trademark Dumont light-blue eyes. The older woman was the epitome of poise. Maggie suspected the woman's spine knew no other position than stick straight. She was beautiful in an intimidating way. The princess, equally beautiful, wore an expression of mild amusement, but the man standing behind the women was fully disapproving.

The beagle dashed out of the closet and immediately puddled on the marble floor, and Maggie knew she was toast.

"What is a dog doing in the palace, Monsier Faus?" the queen asked the man behind her. "The palace does not allow pets."

Maggie's heart stopped at the man's name. This was the advisor who had been a royal pain to Michel.

Monsieur continued to look on with disapproval. "Several events outside palace protocol have taken place during your absence. I feel it is my responsibility to inform you."

Maggie fought the urge to bite the man's leg. She shot to her feet, then quickly bowed. "Your Majesty, I'm responsible for the dog. I gave it to Prince Maximillian as a reward for his preparation for Marceau's Citizenship Day. The prince did not approve. In fact, he fired me," she invented, determined to protect Michel. She searched for the appropriate word. "For—"

"Insubordination. No surprise there," Michelina

said, and Maggie blessed the woman a thousand times over for filling in her blank. She bent down to pet the puppy. "Cute dog. I always wanted one, but *my mother* wouldn't allow it."

"Your Highness, about the other violations of protocol," Faus began.

Violations. Maggie gulped. What a strong word to describe a frog, a turtle and a photo op. "Your Majesty, I'm certain your son is eager to be the first to greet you and meet with you. He is, after all, your heir," she said with an edge directed at Faus. "Marceau's heir."

The queen gave Maggie a hard look. "Your name and position," she demanded, more than asked, but Maggie was growing accustomed to the routine.

"Maggie Gillian. I am," she said, then corrected herself. "I was Prince Maximillian's summer tutor."

"From America," the queen said.

"Yes, Your Majesty."

"Why am I not surprised," she murmured with a sigh.

"I can read now," Max said in a still, small voice.

The queen's eyes softened just a shade. "You can?"

He nodded and bowed. "Yes, ma'am. I can read now. I couldn't before," he confessed.

Maggie bit her lip at his courage. She was so proud of him she couldn't speak.

"If you've done such a good job with Maximillian, then why is Prince Michel firing you?" she demanded of Maggie.

"The puppy," Maggie reminded the woman. "But it's time for me to go back to America."

"I want her to stay," Max said.

The queen raised her eyebrows. "That is for Prince Michel to decide. Now you and your tutor must clean up the dog's mess while I talk to Prince Michel."

"Your Majesty," Faus began.

"Later," the queen said, and left the rest of them in her wake.

Michel answered the queen's summons and dipped his head as he entered her office. "Welcome home, Your Majesty," he said.

"Thank you," she said. "Faus met me at the door and was eager to give me a report, but Michelina and I happened upon a dog on the way to our quarters."

Michel tensed.

"A dog who puddled on the floor, plus your son and a red-haired woman with the worst curtsy I've ever witnessed. She said you fired her for insubordination, and when Faus said he wanted to give me a report, she had the cheek to advise me that the proper course would be to meet with my son." The queen gave an indignant huff. "This had better be good."

Michel couldn't stop a rush of warmth toward Maggie. She would sacrifice herself to protect him. The knowledge gave him strength. "Which would you like me to address first?"

"The palace does not permit dogs," she said with implacable firmness. "The dog must go."

Round one. "Elvis sleeps in the basement, and Maximillian will be responsible for his care."

The queen blinked. "Elvis," she echoed in disbelief.

Michel bit the inside of his cheek to keep from laughing. "Maximillian named the dog."

"Elvis," she repeated. "You must not have heard me. The dog must go."

"The dog will stay," Michel said calmly.

The queen turned deadly silent. "Are you defying my authority?"

"No. I'm merely exercising my authority as a father, as any father in Marceau has the right to do," he said meeting her gaze head-on.

He watched his mother digest his words. "Michel, may I speak frankly?"

"Yes, ma'am."

"I'm getting too old for this. I don't want to rule anymore. I want to be a grandmother. I want to step down, but I want you to be married first. How was the visit with Isabella?"

Round two. "Isabella is a lovely woman, but we aren't well suited."

"But I thought—" The queen broke off and frowned. "Didn't you find her attractive?"

"She's beautiful," he said.

"Did she offend you in some way?"

"Not at all," he said, thinking of how many times Maggie had disagreed with him. "We simply are not well-suited. I'm not a twenty-year-old anymore. I've grown more opinionated about this matter."

"Picky," she said and sighed. Her weariness and age suddenly showed to Michel. "I'll have to think on this. In the meantime, is Maximillian prepared for Citizenship Day?"

"Yes."

"Good. If this tutor has been so successful with Maximillian, perhaps you should reconsider firing her." She winced. "It would appear that she has good intentions if not always sound judgment. Anything else I should know?"

"There was a rock slide on the road to the north," he said.

The queen tensed. "Injuries?"

"Yes, but no fatalities."

She eased slightly. "Good."

"Nicholas helped attend to the injuries. He used an assumed name."

She closed her eyes for a moment. "He's home."

"Temporarily," Michel said. "And he got a haircut."

She opened her eyes and smiled slightly. "Crumbs from heaven."

"Prince Maximillian paid a brief visit to the clinic housing some of the victims and gave away a few books. A photograph was taken and published in the newspaper. The palace PR department was ecstatic."

"But you weren't," she said. "Anything else?"

Round three. "I'd like to offer Faus an ambassadorship to Switzerland," he said. Actually he preferred sending Faus to Antarctica, but was trying to honor the man's years of service.

The queen did a double take. "I'll take that under advisement. You should remember that a thorn in one's side keeps one humble," she said, and narrowed her eyes. "I suspect there's more."

Round four. "Prince Maximillian will begin swimming lessons next week after Citizenship Day."

The queen's face hardened. "Absolutely not."

"Again," he said as gently as he could, "as a father, I must make wise choices for my son."

"I cannot permit this," she said, her eyes full of fear.

"You must."

She took a breath. "As a leader how can you

make this choice? How can you allow your son to be placed in danger?''

''As a leader, I cannot allow my heir to be ruled by fear or ignorance.''

She took another breath. ''Tell me there's nothing else.''

Final round. ''There is a woman I am considering marrying.''

The queen's eyes rounded. ''Oh really. Who is this? Have I met her? Tell me she's European.''

''You've met her, but she's not European. She is Mademoiselle Maggie Gillian,'' he said, and felt a flood of freedom flow through his veins at the announcement.

The queen gaped at him. ''God save me. The tutor,'' she said. ''The fired tutor responsible for the dog in the palace. The American tutor with the terrible curtsy.'' She sucked in a breath of shocked disbelief. ''Absolutely not. Over my dead body.''

Michel swallowed a smile. ''You have time to think about it. Perhaps after you have an opportunity to rest.'' He hadn't seen his mother this rattled in a very long time. He felt a wave of pity for her. ''How was Michelina?''

The queen pressed her lips together as if to stifle a sigh. ''Hellacious,'' she said. ''Your sister is impossible. When you take the throne, you must also take control of her.''

In your dreams, Michel thought, and felt an impulse he hadn't had in years. He could almost hear Maggie hounding him to follow his instincts. "Mother," he said, and she glanced at him in surprise, "welcome home." And he kissed her cheek.

The following afternoon Maggie found an unobtrusive place toward the front of the crowd waiting for Prince Maximillian's appearance. With a mixture of pride in Max and heartache at the knowledge that she would be leaving the next day, she stood with the citizens of Marceau.

The queen, decked out in robe and crown, offered a brief greeting to the warm crowd. Maggie sensed a great affection and respect for the queen. There was, after all, a lot to admire. The woman had given birth to seven children and survived the loss of a child and her husband. She'd ruled under the threat of war and economic devastation and somehow managed to keep her country at peace.

Maggie caught sight of Michel's brother, Auguste, standing to the side, the military second in command. His wife and two little girls sat behind him.

Michel approached the microphone, and the crowd erupted in applause. Her heart clenched at the sight of him. He emanated power and strength in public and private. In private, though, she had seen and loved another side of him.

Her throat grew tight with emotion. She wished

things were different. She wished she could stay even though it would be foolish for her future. Francois, however, had confided to her just this morning that rumors about her and Michel had begun to swirl around the palace. Pretty soon there would be a leak, and the press would find out, and Michel would lose his precious privacy.

Her eyes stung with unshed tears. She couldn't be a part of hurting him. She wouldn't be. That was the reason she would finish packing her clothes this afternoon and be gone tomorrow. She had given what she could, not near enough to last a lifetime, but she couldn't stay any longer without causing damage.

"Good citizens of Marceau, it is my great honor to introduce Prince Maximillian, who will deliver a special message on this day set aside to honor the great citizens of Marceau."

Maggie watched Max approach the microphone and search the crowd. She smiled just in case he was looking for her and prayed that he would be okay.

He took a big breath and began to speak. He delivered the speech perfectly, and she let out a whoop of happiness at the end. She gave him a thumbs-up. He must have caught sight of her because he smiled and return the signal.

"Do you know the young prince?" a man in front of her asked as the crowd went wild.

"Kinda sorta," she said, beaming when the crowd started chanting, "Encore, encore!"

"Darn, we didn't plan for this," she muttered.

Max stepped in front of the microphone again and the crowd quieted. "The citizens of Marceau *rock!*"

Maggie laughed, and the crowd once again roared its approval. She gave another thumbs-up and the man in front of her snapped a picture. Max echoed the signal, and the man took his picture, too.

Fear knotted her stomach. She watched the man turn toward her, and she stumbled toward the back of the crowd. Michel would not be pleased, she thought, running as fast as she could. She could only pray her photo wouldn't turn out.

Two hours later Michel, thrilled with his son's success, entered Maggie's room. He picked her up and spun her around. "He was amazing, incredible. The queen still doesn't quite understand the term *rock,* but she's very pleased."

"I'm very glad," she said quietly. "I'm very, very glad for all of you."

Hearing her muted tone, he studied her. "I thought you would want to celebrate. This is a huge success for you, too."

"Max did the work," she said simply.

Confused, Michel glanced around her room and noticed her suitcase on the bed. His gut sank. "Why are you packing?"

She inhaled as if visibly trying to calm herself. "My flight leaves tomorrow."

"Absolutely not," he said.

"My assignment is complete."

"You cannot leave," he told her, struggling with an odd sensation that combined desperation and flat-out denial.

"I must leave," she told him. "Rumors have started about you and me. It's only a matter of time before people outside the palace hear. I can't allow that."

"I'm not afraid of rumors," he said, trying to identify the odd sensation he felt. *Sweating,* he realized in shock. He was sweating. No one made him sweat.

"Not only that, I got caught in another nonboring moment today, and I'm afraid the press will go for the jugular once the photo is out."

Michel paused. "Photo?"

"I was a bit demonstrative when Max gave his speech," she said, biting her lip. "After I screamed and whistled and gave the thumbs-up, a reporter snapped my picture and started asking questions. I ran away," she added quickly. "But..."

A plan came to mind. Michel looked into her green eyes and put his hands on her arms. "Will you do something for me if I ask you?"

He saw the fear in her eyes soften. "I'll do anything except stay," she said.

"Three more days," he said, willing her to agree.

She shook her head, and he began to sweat again. "Bad idea," she said. "I really should go."

"Three days," he repeated. "Is it so much to give out of your life?"

Her eyes grew shiny. "You don't know how hard this is for me," she whispered.

Michel ached for her. He hated seeing her in pain. "Three more days," he repeated.

She nodded. "No more than that," she said, her gaze full of warning. "Absolutely no more than three more days."

He kissed her firmly and pulled back. "Excuse me. I have a pressing meeting, but I want you to come to my quarters later."

Ignoring her protests, he headed down the hall to put the palace PR department to work. After an hour with his top three press aides, he knew he had laid the groundwork for his success. Family demands, however, continued to plague him. Michelina wanted to discuss a way to return to the States. His brother Nicholas was already leaving for a professional symposium. His other brother Jean-Marc had sent a fax requesting the assignment as Marceau's diplomatic representative to the United States.

Everyone wanted to go to America, Michel thought. His mother was going to flip.

The queen insisted on proudly showing pictures of her newest grandchild to all. She was pleased to give a full report on the parents, too: Michel's youngest brother, Alexander, and his wife, Sophia.

By the time he retired to his quarters, Maggie was nowhere in sight. Although he missed her, he knew tomorrow was going to be a very busy day for her. He had big plans for Maggie Gillian. She was damn well going to need her rest.

Eleven

As soon as the morning paper hit the front step, Michel ordered it brought to him. With satisfaction he read of his son's triumph. His heart swelled at the sight of the photos of Max giving the thumbs-up sign and at the sight of sweet Maggie, her love and joy emanating from her eyes.

He pored over the article praising Max and the other article, lower on the page, but still prominent, revealing the impact of Maggie's tutoring on Max. The article detailed her impressive academic credentials. The resourceful reporter had even managed to get quotes from some Marceau citizens who had met Maggie at the library's adult literacy program and the clinic Max had also visited.

Michel knew Max had once been viewed as a sad, lonely child after his mother had died. The people who had felt sorrow for him now shared in his victory. The woman who had helped make it happen was Maggie. Maggie Gillian had just become a national treasure.

Michel downed the last of his coffee and tucked the newspaper under his arm for his meeting with the queen.

The queen tossed him a sideways glance as he entered the room. "I've already read it," she said of the paper.

"Including the article about Maggie," he said.

She nodded regally. "Amazing how the press got access to all that information in such a short time."

"Not really," Michel said. "We have an excellent PR department."

"Michel, she's not right for the job of your wife. Your wife must be poised and self-controlled. She must defer to you and support you in all matters. She must be above reproach. She must respect royal protocol."

He stuck his hands in his pockets. "That's what the advisors have told me for years."

"And the advisors are correct."

"The problem is that the advisors don't have to marry my wife. I do."

The queen absorbed that comment. "I am not at all swayed," she told him. "But I am listening."

He nodded. "I didn't plan to love her and would never have chosen her for my wife."

"Then why do you choose her now?"

He searched for the words. How could he possibly explain this? "She is argumentative," he said, "but I've never met a woman deliver a more sincere apology than Maggie. She's impatient with protocol because she's impatient with anything that interferes with my happiness. She believes I deserve to be happy. She doesn't love me because I'm royalty. She loves me in spite of the fact that I am royalty. She loves Michel," he said, certain he was bungling this.

"She makes my worst day better," he said. "She takes the grind out of ruling. I'm a better man because of her."

The queen silently studied her folded hands. "Your father did that for me. I have missed him," she said, her voice quiet. She lifted her head to gaze at Michel. "I will see her this afternoon," she told him, and Michel knew he was halfway there.

"I still don't understand why your mother wants to see me," Maggie said as Michel led her toward a formal parlor. "She can't stand me."

"She's grateful for your work with Max," Michel said.

"Max did the hard part." She felt a sick feeling as she stopped just outside the parlor door. "Michel, I really don't want to talk to your mother. I'm only going to be here two more days. Can't I go to the beach or something instead?''

"Ma chère, this isn't optional," Michel told her as the assistant opened the door.

Maggie fought a slice of panic. "I don't want to do this," she whispered desperately.

"You'll be fine," he told her, and kissed her.

Maggie tried to draw courage from his strength as she faced the parlor. Inhaling deeply, she told herself she would only have to face the woman once. At least this time she was doing it sans Elvis, the beagle.

She entered the room and dipped her knees in a curtsy. "Your Majesty," she murmured, uncertain whether she was supposed to speak first or wait.

"Please be seated, Mademoiselle Gillian," the queen said waving to the chair opposite her. She nodded to the assistant to pour the tea.

"In the short time you've been here, you've made quite a dramatic impact on my son and grandson. Both sing your praises."

"Prince Max has been a pleasure to work with. He's been an excellent student. He will be a terrific man," she said, knowing the warm spot in her heart for Max would never turn cold.

"Do you love my grandson?" the queen asked bluntly.

"How could anyone not love Max?" she answered with a shrug. "He's smart and funny and curious. He's tough, but he's got a great heart."

"You don't treat him like a prince," the queen observed.

"That's right. He's already got a gazillion people doing that, so I have just tried to treat him like a human being. I think everyone should have at least one person who loves them and treats them like a human being, don't you?"

The queen sipped her tea and appeared to consider her words. "But what of preparing him to rule?"

Maggie took a sip of her tea and set it down. "It depends on what kind of preparation you mean. There are others who can teach him protocol and Prince Michel will make sure Max fulfills tradition at the same time he learns character. Max is really fortunate to have Michel as a father. Michel will make sure Max gets what he needs."

"But what of your contribution to Maximillian?" the queen continued.

Maggie shrugged. "I helped him learn to read and let him see that learning can be fun. I like to think I helped him find some of his power. You see, I'm much more interested in building character than making a prince. Between you and Michel, Max has some pretty big shoes to fill. He will need to be a good human being if he is to be an effective ruler."

"And Prince Michel, how do you view his destiny as ruler of Marceau?"

Maggie found the queen's question odd, but the woman's attitude compelled her to answer. "It's a tough, lonely job with long hours. He's an incredibly intelligent man who is passionate about his vision. Marceau is lucky." She wanted to say, Can I go now?, but she bit her tongue.

"What I wish to know, Mademoiselle Gillian, is why you think you would be the best woman to be the wife of Prince Michel?"

Maggie blinked and felt light-headed. Surely she couldn't have heard correctly. "I'm sorry. Could you repeat the question?"

The queen patiently repeated her question word for word.

Maggie shook her head. "I would be a terrible wife for Michel," she said. "I don't know any of the protocol, and if I did, I'd probably forget it. I argue with him. I wouldn't mind having two or three children, but I'm not interested in having six, with all due respect," she said. "I am much more interested in Michel's happiness than I am interested in the fact that he's a prince. I'm interested in him as a man," she said, having trouble avoiding saying that she loved him. "Plus I would be a rotten princess. I don't know how to curtsy correctly—"

"I have observed," the queen said in a dry voice. "That can be learned. Thank you for coming. You may be excused."

Maggie blinked at the abruptness. "Oh. Well, it was nice meeting you again, Your Majesty," she said, standing and giving another slight bob.

The queen nodded.

Maggie walked to the door. "Goodbye," she said.

"À bientôt, mademoiselle."

Whatever that meant, Maggie thought as the door closed behind her. This was one weird family. She rounded the corner where Michel was leaning against the wall.

He looked at her expectantly. "How did it go?" he asked.

"With all due respect," Maggie said, "your mother is weird. She didn't really thank me for working with Max. She just asked me a lot of odd questions." She tried to shake off the strange conversation. "I think I'm going to the beach for a little while."

"I'll go with you," he said. "The car is waiting."

She searched his gaze. "Are you sure you have time?"

"Yes, of course," he said, as if he was a man of leisure. And Maggie knew he wasn't.

The black limo glided through Marceau's streets to a gated area that led to a private beach. "For security reasons my family uses a private beach on this side of the island."

Extending his hand to her, he guided her through a treed area to the deserted afternoon beach. Maggie inhaled the scent of salt and sea air. "This truly is a beautiful place," she said, thinking she would miss it for far more than its beauty. It was difficult to believe she'd arrived in Marceau just over six weeks ago. She gazed at Michel and memorized his profile with the wind ruffling his dark hair. He appeared deep in thought, yet peaceful. She wanted to seal this moment and every moment she'd shared with him forever in her mind.

The sand was packed down from the recent rain, so she kept her shoes on. "I'd like to take back a couple of shells," she told him, and walked to the edge of the water.

As she knelt to pick up three shells, she felt Michel's hands on her shoulders. "There's something I must discuss with you."

Her stomach turned a flip at his tone. She glanced up at him. His solemn expression seemed ominous. "Is something wrong?"

He nodded. "I have a problem and I need your help."

She immediately stood. "What is it?" she asked, unable to imagine him needing her advice for anything other than Max's education.

He touched a wild strand of her hair. "I'm preparing for an extremely high-level negotiation, and I find I don't have much to offer the other party."

"Are you negotiating for a special service or alliance, some sort of trade agreement?"

"Yes," he said.

"All three," she said, bemused. "Well, what do you want from the other party?"

"Everything," he said. "I want total commitment, loyalty and access."

"And you can't offer the same?"

"To a degree, but as you know, I was born with a prior commitment," he said with a wry grin.

Perplexed, Maggie shrugged. "It doesn't sound like a very equitable agreement."

"It won't always be," he agreed. "I could provide a monetary exchange."

"That might help," she said.

"But the other party isn't interested in money," he said, and his gaze was so compelling Maggie couldn't have looked away from him if her life depended on it. "Not interested in diamonds or titles."

Her heart pounded in her chest. Her mind slowly put two and two together, but she couldn't begin to speak.

"I could promise you jewels and wealth," he told her. "I could promise that people would bow to you, but none of that would win you," he said. "I can't promise that you'll be my top priority every minute of every day. As you've said, I have a job with terrible hours."

He raked a hand through his hair and swore. "I've never wanted a woman more in my life, and I'm totally botching this. Do you know that you are the only woman who has ever made me sweat?"

Maggie's head was spinning, but his last question got through. "I am?" she asked, biting her lip. "Little Maggie Gillian makes the mighty Prince Michel sweat?" she ventured, incredulous.

He looked more tense than a fully stretched bow. Although her own chest was tight with emotion and her mind was filled with confusion, she took his hand. "Maybe it would be better if you didn't treat this like a negotiation. Maybe it would be better if you just said what you feel. Because it sounds like the most important thing you're offering is your-self.''

''I love you,'' he said.

Maggie locked her suddenly liquid knees.

''You've been a haven I didn't know I needed. I want to be the same for you. I have many people who are paid to protect me. You would protect me without compensation. I can promise the same for you. You've given my son new life. You fill me up when I feel used up.'' He narrowed his eyes in con-centration as if the words were difficult to find. ''You're the one woman I want to know and who I want to know me. Please be my wife.''

Maggie grew light-headed. Tears filled her eyes, and she covered them with her hand. A sob welled up in her throat and she couldn't contain it. She hadn't dared to dream Michel would ask such a thing.

''Why are you crying?''

She shook her head helplessly. ''I...I...'' She sobbed again. ''I didn't know you felt that way about me. I want to be the woman for you.'' She sniffed. ''This is going to sound crazy. I want to take care of you, but you need a wife who is dif-ferent from me.''

Michel gently shook her shoulders. ''Don't you understand? No other woman has even thought she wanted to take care of me. You are more rare than the finest precious stone. There's no other woman who can help me be the best man I can be, the best ruler I can be.''

Maggie felt another storm of emotion rage inside her. She swiped at her cheeks and sniffed. ''Oh, God, but I would be such a lousy royal.''

''You wouldn't be the traditional royal wife. That's not necessarily bad. We can work that out.''

She shook her head, full of doubt, still afraid to hope. ''I don't know, Michel. If this were just about you and me, the answer would be easy.''

''Marriage is rarely just about two people. More is involved. Our life together will be a challenge,'' he said. ''But you are worth it to me. You must decide if I'm worth it to you.''

That night Michel's family was apparently holding a meeting. Maggie had no idea why. She had her own life crisis staring her in the face. Unable to sleep, she stole outside to the courtyard and drank in the peaceful darkness.

Moments later Michel joined her, still dressed.

She gave a questioning glance at his attire. ''Late family meeting,'' she said.

He nodded. ''We received some pretty amazing news. A letter with postmarks from about fifteen countries arrived for my mother today. It was forwarded from several places. It had to be over fifteen years old.''

''Wow. Do you know where it originated?''

He shook his head and stuck a fist in his pocket, his gaze full of turmoil. ''There are more unan-

swered than answered questions. There was a lock
of hair and a button enclosed with the letter. The
person who wrote the letter said my brother Jacques
Simon did not drown when he was three.''

She gaped at him. ''What?''

''Jacques's body was never found. There's no signature on the letter. Whoever wrote it said that
Jacques survived falling overboard during the storm,
and he was picked up by a fisherman, a childless
fisherman.''

Amazement warred with doubt and hope on
Michel's face. ''Do you think he could still be
alive?'' she asked.

''We don't know, but we have reason to hope.
The hair has already gone to a special lab. My
mother remembers the button from Jacques's coat.''

''How is she…your mother?''

''She fainted,'' he said in disbelief. ''I've never
known her to faint. If Jacques is alive, we must find
him.''

Michel appeared to want to go in search of him
right this minute. ''But not tonight,'' she said, skimming her hand over his arm.

He met her gaze and took a deep breath. He nodded. ''Not tonight.''

She smiled. ''You've had a full day. Engineered
the public relations miracle of turning me into a heroine,'' she began.

His eyes glinted with pleasure. ''You read the article.''

''You wrote it,'' she said.

"Not technically," he said. "I just provided a little guidance and a few leads."

"Uh-huh," she said at the understatement. "You also bulldozed your mother into approving me, proposed marriage and found out your dead brother may be alive."

His gaze asked the question, but he restrained himself from speaking it. She could spend a lifetime seducing that man past his restraint. "It occurred to me that we have never danced."

He glanced around the courtyard, then pulled her into his arms. She felt his heart beating against her cheek, she again heard his unvoiced question and closed her eyes.

Her heart was full and achy with the prospect of the decision she was about to make. "It also occurred to me that I've never been on a picnic with you. Or a boat for that matter. I've also never made love with you in your office."

He pulled his head back and gazed at her. "You're making me sweat again."

A thrill raced down her spine.

She swallowed over the lump in her throat and the tinge of fear that she was inadequate. "I think I want to make you sweat for a long time," she whispered.

"How long?"

"Forever."

Epilogue

Six months later, on a bright sunny morning, the minister of the official church of Marceau pronounced them husband and wife in front of five hundred of Michel's close friends and family along with Maggie's loved ones. This was the royal version of a small ceremony.

During the months of their engagement, Maggie's doubts had fallen, one by one, under Michel's steady love and determination. Surprisingly enough, Francois had become an advocate and friend, filling her in on proper protocol—some of which she followed and some of which she did not and never would.

Michel lowered his head and took her face in his

hands. "This is the happiest day of my life," he said, and kissed her.

With her husband's mouth on hers, she heard bells throughout the city begin to ring. Marceau was pleased.

After an elaborate six-hour reception, Maggie and Michel stole away to his yacht and left Marceau and Max in the caring hands of the queen. The queen planned to officially hand the throne to Michel soon.

Maggie stood in her husband's arms on the deck as the sun began its slow descent. She turned, sliding her arms around him and burying her face in his chest. He gave a rumble of approval. "Don't you want to watch the sunset?"

"I'd rather watch you," she said, looking up at him.

"How does it feel to be a princess?" he asked with a teasing light in his eyes.

"Oh, you're not going to start that already, are you?"

He chuckled. "But, Your Highness," he continued.

She swatted him. "Oh, shut up."

"Whatever pleases Her Highness," he said, and she groaned.

She met his gaze. "You know I've never made love to you on a yacht," she said.

His eyes darkened. "I can change that."

She nodded, feeling the anticipation inside her already begin to build. "The queen told me that you would always belong to the people."

With the wind whipping through his hair, he was thoughtful for a long moment, then a glint of sexy mischief crossed his eyes. "Parts of me will always belong exclusively to you."

"Oh, really," she said, unable to keep from smiling. She didn't think she'd stopped smiling all day. "What parts would those be?"

He picked her up in his arms and carried her toward the bedroom. "Let me show you." His eyes were full of promises she knew they both would keep.

*   *   *   *   *

*Be sure to watch for more
compelling stories by Leanne Banks
involving*
THE ROYAL DUMONTS
*coming soon in 2002
And don't miss Leanne Banks launching
Desire's brand-new 12-book continuity*
DYNASTIES: THE CONNELLYS
*On sale in January 2002 from
Silhouette Desire*

THE FORTUNES OF TEXAS

invite you to meet

THE LOST HEIRS

Silhouette Desire's scintillating
new miniseries, featuring the beloved

FORTUNES OF TEXAS

and six of your favorite authors.

A Most Desirable M.D.—June 2001
by Anne Marie Winston (SD #1371)

The Pregnant Heiress—July 2001
by Eileen Wilks (SD #1378)

Baby of Fortune—August 2001
by Shirley Rogers (SD #1384)

Fortune's Secret Daughter—September 2001
by Barbara McCauley (SD #1390)

Her Boss's Baby—October 2001
by Cathleen Galitz (SD #1396)

Did You Say Twins?!—December 2001
by Maureen Child (SD #1408)

And be sure to watch for *Gifts of Fortune*,
Silhouette's exciting new single title,
on sale November 2001

*Don't miss these unforgettable romances…
available at your favorite retail outlet.*

Where love comes alive™

Visit Silhouette at www.eHarlequin.com   SDFOT

CALL THE ONES YOU LOVE OVER THE HOLIDAYS!

Save $25 off future book purchases when you buy any four Harlequin® or Silhouette® books in October, November and December 2001,

PLUS

receive a phone card good for 15 minutes of long-distance calls to anyone you want in North America!

WHAT AN INCREDIBLE DEAL!

Just fill out this form and attach 4 proofs of purchase (cash register receipts) from October, November and December 2001 books, and Harlequin Books will send you a coupon booklet worth a total savings of $25 off future purchases of Harlequin® and Silhouette® books, AND a 15-minute phone card to call the ones you love, anywhere in North America.

Please send this form, along with your cash register receipts as proofs of purchase, to:
In the USA: Harlequin Books, P.O. Box 9057, Buffalo, NY 14269-9057
In Canada: Harlequin Books, P.O. Box 622, Fort Erie, Ontario L2A 5X3
Cash register receipts must be dated no later than December 31, 2001.
Limit of 1 coupon booklet and phone card per household.
Please allow 4-6 weeks for delivery.

**I accept your offer! Enclosed are 4 proofs of purchase.
Please send me my coupon booklet
and a 15-minute phone card:**

Name: _____

Address: _____ City: _____

State/Prov.: _____ Zip/Postal Code: _____

Account Number (if available): _____

---

097 KJB DAGL
PHQ4013

If you enjoyed what you just read,
then we've got an offer you can't resist!

Take 2 bestselling love stories FREE!

Plus get a FREE surprise gift!

Clip this page and mail it to Silhouette Reader Service™

IN U.S.A.	**IN CANADA**
3010 Walden Ave.	P.O. Box 609
P.O. Box 1867	Fort Erie, Ontario
Buffalo, N.Y. 14240-1867	L2A 5X3

YES! Please send me 2 free Silhouette Desire® novels and my free surprise gift. After receiving them, if I don't wish to receive anymore, I can return the shipping statement marked cancel. If I don't cancel, I will receive 6 brand-new novels every month, before they're available in stores! In the U.S.A., bill me at the bargain price of $3.34 plus 25¢ shipping and handling per book and applicable sales tax, if any*. In Canada, bill me at the bargain price of $3.74 plus 25¢ shipping and handling per book and applicable taxes**. That's the complete price and a savings of at least 10% off the cover prices—what a great deal! I understand that accepting the 2 free books and gift places me under no obligation ever to buy any books. I can always return a shipment and cancel at any time. Even if I never buy another book from Silhouette, the 2 free books and gift are mine to keep forever.

225 SEN DFNS
326 SEN DFNT

Name	(PLEASE PRINT)	
Address	Apt.#	
City	State/Prov.	Zip/Postal Code

* Terms and prices subject to change without notice. Sales tax applicable in N.Y.
** Canadian residents will be charged applicable provincial taxes and GST.
All orders subject to approval. Offer limited to one per household and not valid to current Silhouette Desire® subscribers.
® are registered trademarks of Harlequin Enterprises Limited.

DES01   ©1998 Harlequin Enterprises Limited

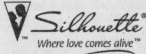